'Liam?' Jennifer leaned closer and raised her voice.

'Liam? It's Dr Jennifer Tremaine. Open your eyes for me.'

'He's not responsive.' The deep male voice came from the back seat of the car. 'Except to painful stimuli.'

Jennifer nodded. Liam's mouth was closed around the end of a plastic OP airway.

'Here's the oxygen.' A mask was passed in beside Jennifer. 'It's running on fifteen litres.'

Jennifer fitted the mask to Liam's face. As she pulled the elastic strap behind his head her hands brushed the arm of the man still supporting Liam's head. She glanced up, registering the stranger's appearance for the first time. She blinked and stared, her jaw dropping. The man smiled without amusement.

'Hello, Jennifer. Fancy meeting you here.'

'Andrew!'

Alison Roberts was born in New Zealand, and says, 'I lived in London and Washington DC as a child, and began my working career as a primary school teacher. A lifelong interest in medicine was fostered by my doctor and nurse parents, flatting with doctors and physiotherapists on leaving home, and marriage to a house surgeon who is now a consultant cardiologist. I have also worked as a cardiology technician and research assistant. My husband's medical career took us to Glasgow for two years, which was an ideal place and time to start my writing career. I now live in Christchurch, New Zealand, with my husband, daughter and various pets.'

Recent titles by the same author:

DOCTOR IN DANGER
EMOTIONAL RESCUE
NURSE IN NEED

RIVALS IN PRACTICE

BY
ALISON ROBERTS

MILLS & BOON®

First published in Great Britain 2002
Large Print edition 2002
Harlequin Mills & Boon Limited,
Eton House, 18-24 Paradise Road,
Richmond, Surrey TW9 1SR

© Alison Roberts 2002

ISBN 0 263 17318 6

Set in Times Roman 16½ on 18 pt.
17-1102-47273

Printed and bound in Great Britain
by Antony Rowe Ltd, Chippenham, Wiltshire

CHAPTER ONE

THE crack split the airwaves as unnervingly as gunfire.

'My God, what was *that*?' The fear in the woman's eyes had nothing to do with the reason she was lying on a hospital bed.

Dr Jennifer Tremaine turned away from the window with a reassuring smile. 'Nobody's been shot, Liz. It's just a branch coming down on that old twisted willow by the front gate.'

Elizabeth Bailey settled back onto her pillows reluctantly. 'Must have been a pretty big branch.'

'It was. I think some of these wind gusts are getting over a hundred kilometres an hour.'

A nurse smoothed the final piece of clean linen into the bassinet with a satisfied pat. Then she straightened, turning suddenly as a fresh gust of wind rattled the window viciously and sent droplets of water against the glass with enough force to sound like a shower of small pebbles.

'I thought this was supposed to be the tail end of that southerly storm.' The nurse, Wendy Granger, peered out of the window. 'It looks a lot closer to the head end to me.'

'At least we had plenty of warning. The fishing boats should all be in and they closed the school early.' Jennifer Tremaine frowned as she picked up the chart lying on the end of Elizabeth's bed. The small rural community of Akaroa, nestled into a peninsula on the South Island of New Zealand, wasn't used to winter weather of such severity but preparations had been a focus all day. The young doctor's immediate concerns were much closer. If she needed back-up for any complications with Elizabeth's labour, the nearest large centre was Christchurch. Evacuation by air was clearly out of the question already, and even in good weather transport by road took an hour and a half.

'That branch has blocked the front driveway completely,' Wendy announced. 'I hope no one's been injured.'

'You and me both.' Jennifer glanced at her watch. 'I must ring home. I want to check that the children are all back from school safely.' She frowned again, her attention still on her watch. 'It's over ten minutes since your last contraction, Liz. You're slowing down again.'

'Oh, no! Is this going to be another false alarm?'

'I guess we'll have to wait and see.' Jennifer smiled at her patient. 'One thing's for sure, we won't be sending you home in a hurry in this sort of weather. As I explained to you yesterday, the position your baby is in is likely to make the first stage of labour quite a lot longer than usual. The backache you're getting is the other major disadvantage.'

Liz sighed heavily. 'Trust Peter's child to be difficult before it's even born. Like father, like son—or daughter,' she added.

'Have you heard from Peter again?'

'He rang half an hour ago. The airport at Dunedin is closed because of the weather. There's no chance of him getting back tonight. I hope it *is* another false alarm.'

'How's your back feeling?'

'Sore, but no worse than it's been since I came in yesterday morning. What was it you called the position?'

'It's called a right occiputo posterior position. It means that the baby's facing the front. The most normal presentation is when the back of the head is pressing on the abdominal wall. The back of your baby's head is pressing against your sacrum.' Jennifer smiled wryly. 'Commonly known as ''backache labour'', I'm afraid.'

'What's going to happen?'

'The baby will most likely turn itself around at the very end of the first stage or the beginning of the second and then things will go a lot more smoothly and quickly.'

'How long will it take?'

'I can't say,' Jennifer apologised. 'You're still only three centimetres dilated so we can't even be sure whether labour is established yet or not. Try moving around as much as you can for the moment. If you stay upright, it will tip the baby down and might ease the pressure on the small of your back. Kneeling, being on your hands and knees and lying on your side, curled up, might help the pain and encourage the rotation of the baby. We'll give you a hot pack, and ask Wendy for a massage any time you like.' Jennifer turned to her nurse. 'Why don't you put the kettle on first, Wendy? I think we could all use a cup of tea. I'm just going to pop up to the office and give Saskia a ring. She should be back from collecting the children by now.'

The wide, wood-panelled hallway and the impressive height of the ceiling could have graced a stately home. The small hospital had been built in an era when function and budgets couldn't overrule aesthetic considerations. More recent additions were modern, and Jennifer was proud of their maternity suite, treatment and consulting rooms but she loved the older part of the hospital. The rooms were spacious, most opened onto verandahs that were more than welcome in the hot, summer months and the marginal plumbing could be forgiven because they were never stretched to use their entire ten-bed capacity.

The hospital office was near the front of the old weatherboard building and the room was large enough to accommodate Jennifer, her older partner, Dr Brian Wallace, and the secretary who worked weekday mornings. The ancient carpet was still thick enough to muffle the sound of Jennifer's approach and she stopped in the doorway with a small groan of dismay. The room had enough windows to give a clear view of the worsening storm and the impressive pile of debris from the willow tree could be seen covering the driveway, but Jennifer wasn't looking outside. Her dismay was directed at the man sitting in front of a computer screen.

'How bad is it, Brian?'

Brian Wallace shoved a desk drawer shut with a startled bang. 'Bloody awful,' he growled. 'I've lost the report I'd just finished because of some power disruption and the damned thing's vanished. I'm sure I saved it.'

'That's not what I'm talking about.' Jennifer crossed the room quickly. 'I saw you drop your spray into the drawer. Why didn't you tell me you had your angina back again?'

The older man sighed with resignation. 'I didn't want to worry you, Jen.' He looked up and smiled. 'It's not so bad—really.'

'And it came on while you were sitting here quietly at the computer?'

'It came on thanks to the stress these infernal machines are capable of generating. I've spent a week on that report. We should never have tried to get so modern. We did just fine in my day before technology started to take over. I want my typewriter back.'

'Oh, sure.' Jennifer grinned. 'You use the Internet more than any of us do. You'd be totally lost without it.' Her smile faded. Jennifer wasn't going to allow complete distraction. 'Come with me. I want to do a twelve-lead ECG.'

Brian scowled. 'Let me have another go at finding this report first. I'll reboot the computer and see if that helps.'

Another loud crack outside made Jennifer flinch. The lights in the office flickered, went out for several seconds, then came on again with slightly diminished strength. The menu on the screen in front of Brian vanished.

'Shut down,' Jennifer advised firmly. 'It looks like our emergency generator has kicked in and the less power we use, the better. The computer's out of bounds.'

'So's the ECG machine, then.'

'It's battery-powered,' Jennifer reminded her partner crisply. Her expression softened. 'Please, Brian, let me check you over.'

The older doctor complied reluctantly and Jennifer's smile was sympathetic as she led the way down the dark hallway towards the consulting room. Brian Wallace was well into his sixties and probably should have retired two years ago after suffering his first heart attack. Like herself, Brian had been born and raised on the peninsula but it had been his first choice of career to come back here to practise medicine and become an integral part of the small community.

Jennifer's return hadn't been entirely voluntary and her time here as a doctor couldn't begin to compare with Brian's years of service, yet she could already feel the strands of the web the ties created. And they weren't unpleasant ties. The bond was protective as well as demanding. She was a part of so many people's lives. A piece of the fabric of this old building and an equal partner of this GP who had been her friend and mentor for as long as she could remember.

The ECG was reassuring. 'There's no sign of any ST depression or other changes.' Jennifer showed the trace to Brian. 'How's the chest pain at the moment?'

'Gone.'

'Did it feel the same as your previous angina?'

'Pretty much.'

'Any associated symptoms?'

'No.'

'Have you had your aspirin today?'

'Yes, Doctor.' Brian smiled at Jennifer. 'Can I go now?'

'No. I want to take your blood pressure and listen to your chest. If they're OK then you can go. Home—for a rest.'

'It's only three p.m.'

'It's dark enough to be six p.m. and I want you safely home before this storm gets any worse.' Jennifer wrapped the blood-pressure cuff around her colleague's arm.

'We might get extra work.'

'If we do, Wendy and I will cope.' Jennifer reached for the stethoscope hanging around her neck. 'We've only got the two inpatients and Lizzie's labour could well be another false alarm.'

'Well, Wendy's an excellent nurse and I have complete faith in you to cope with anything that needs a doctor.' Brian looked thoughtful. 'And I did promise to check on Jack Currie's ulcer on the way home.'

Jennifer sighed. 'And how many other house calls did you promise to make?' She released the valve on the bulb. 'Your blood pressure's fine. One-forty over ninety.' She placed the disc of the stethoscope on Brian's chest. 'Take a few deep breaths for me.'

The pot of tea was cold by the time Jennifer arrived in the hospital kitchen. She threw a tea-bag into a mug and waited for the kettle to boil again. Wendy came into the kitchen carrying a tray of empty cups and saucers.

'Mrs D. says she wants another biscuit.' Wendy reached for a tin on the shelf above the toaster. 'And she's already had two!'

'The storm's not bothering her, then?'

'I don't think she's noticed.'

Jennifer grinned. Mrs Dobson had become a long-term inpatient. At ninety-seven, she required more medical attention than the local rest home was able to manage, and it had seemed cruel to send her out of the area she had lived in all her life even though she was now often unaware of her surroundings.

'How's Lester?'

'Quiet. He was asleep so I didn't disturb him.'

'Pain relief must be working, then.' Jennifer added a spoonful of sugar to her tea. Lester Booth was suffering from an extremely painful dose of shingles. 'What about Liz?'

'The contractions are following the same pattern. One strong one and then one really feeble one.' Wendy was stacking cups and saucers into the dishwasher. 'She's really fed up and her back pain is getting worse.'

'Have you checked the foetal heartbeat?'

Wendy nodded. 'Nothing's changed. There's no sign of foetal distress.' She grinned at Jennifer. 'Only the maternal variety.'

Jennifer sipped her tea thoughtfully. 'At this rate Liz is going to be worn out well before we get anywhere near the second stage. If I'd sent her into town yesterday she could have been managed more effectively. They could have speeded things up and done a Caesarean if a forceps delivery failed.'

'Liz wanted to wait to give Peter a chance to get home,' Wendy added. 'She was quite pleased when things ground to a halt. Are we likely to run into trouble, do you think?'

'I hope not. It's been a while since I did a forceps rotation and delivery, though.' Jennifer glanced towards the small kitchen window as a wave of hail assaulted the glass. 'I'm worried about the road being cut off. Having that on top of a potential complication makes us feel rather isolated. Let's just hope the baby decides to co-operate and turn itself around.'

Wendy followed her glance with a grimace. 'It's probably snowing on the hilltop by now.' She looked at her watch. 'I'd better go and check on Liz after I've given this to Mrs D.' Wendy picked up the plate with the chocolate biscuit. 'Then I'll take Brian a cup of tea. He wasn't in the office when I went past.'

'I've sent him home.' Jennifer caught Wendy's surprised expression and smiled a trifle grimly. 'He's getting angina again.'

'Oh, no!' The biscuit was in danger of sliding off the plate. 'How bad is it?'

'Hard to know. I suspect Brian hasn't lost his touch at hiding symptoms. I checked him out and I'll do another ECG in the morning, but I didn't want him here just in case things do get busy.'

A faint noise reached the women above the howl of the midwinter storm. A noise that rose and fell with an easily recognised urgency. The warning siren was used to call the local volunteer fire officers in to their station. It was unlikely that their fire-fighting skills would be required right now, however. Far more likely that their role as first responders for ambulance or rescue work was being summoned. Even while the noise was being registered in the kitchen, a much closer signal sounded.

'That's the surgery bell. Shall I go?' Mrs D.'s biscuit was abandoned on the bench.

'No, I'll go.' Jennifer tipped out the rest of her tea. 'You stay with Liz.' She looked over her shoulder as she moved to the door. 'And could you ring home for me when you've got a minute? I still haven't checked on the children.'

The large man standing in the tiny waiting room was wearing an oilskin parka that streamed water onto the linoleum floor. He held one hand clutched to his chest and well-diluted blood was staining the rapidly growing puddle. 'John! What's happened?' Jennifer held open the door of the treatment room. 'Come straight in here.'

'It's a bit of a mess, Doc.' John Bellamy sat down heavily on a chair as Jennifer pulled gloves on and reached for a pack of sterile dressings. 'I was just making sure the boat was secure and this wave rolled right over the deck. I landed in my tackle box.' His face twisted as Jennifer moved his hand to place it on a towel on the bed beside him. She pulled the head of the angle lamp out from the wall and clicked on the light. 'I got one of the damned hooks out but there's another one that's too deep.'

'Sure is.' Jennifer looked at the fish hook buried in the calloused pad below John's thumb. 'And you've got a nasty tear where you pulled the other one out. It's going to need a stitch or two. Let's get your coat off and make you a bit more comfortable first.'

'No point in getting dry.' John shook his head firmly. 'I need to get back and keep an eye on the boat. The tide's not full in yet and we've got waves breaking on the road already.'

Jennifer was drawing up local anaesthetic into a syringe. 'It's going to be too dangerous to be anywhere near the boats, then.' She looked at her patient with concern. 'You're not thinking of getting back on board, I hope.'

John shook his head wearily, releasing more droplets of water from his grizzled hair. 'I just need to watch,' he said quietly. 'That's my livelihood out there.'

'I know.' Jennifer's tone was sympathetic. 'Let's hope things don't get any worse.'

The surgery bell rang again just as Jennifer eased the fish hook from the incision she had made with a scalpel. She pressed a sterile gauze pad over the wound. 'Hold that on for a second, John. I'd better see who that is.'

Two women stood in the waiting room. The younger woman looked anxious. 'Mum's had a fall, Dr Tremaine.'

'I couldn't see a thing when the lights went out!' The older woman sounded annoyed. 'I tripped over the coffee-table.'

'Were you knocked out?'

'No, but I've cut my leg and you know what my skin's like.'

Jennifer nodded. Edith Turner had been on steroids for years to treat her lung condition. Even a slight knock could tear her papery skin badly. Judging by the blood-soaked towel around her lower leg, this accident had been more than a slight knock. She touched the towel to find the stain almost dry.

'It's stopped bleeding, anyway. Take a seat in the consulting room and I'll be with you in a couple of minutes. I've just got a few stitches and a dressing to take care of.' Jennifer was debating whether to open the internal door from the waiting room to call for Wendy's assistance when the outside door opened again.

'The front driveway is completely blocked!' a cheerful voice informed Jennifer. 'So I had to come in this way.'

'Margaret!' Jennifer was delighted to see another of her senior nurses. The uniform the older woman was wearing was a surprise. 'You're on night duty. You're not due in for hours yet.'

'Thought you might need some extra help what with this weather.' Margaret Coates pulled a clear plastic hood clear of her grey hair.

'You're an angel,' Jennifer told her. 'Can you take Edith in to the consulting room and have a look at her leg? You might need to soak that towel off. I've got a bit of stitching to finish in the treatment room.'

The last stitch in John's palm was being tied when Wendy came into the room. 'Contractions are back to ten minutes apart,' she reported to Jennifer. 'Liz is asking for some pain relief.'

'I'll go and see her. Could you dress John's hand? Put a plastic bag over it all when you've finished so it doesn't get wet. John wants to go and have another look at his boat.' Jennifer stripped off her gloves and stood up. 'Did you get hold of Saskia?'

'Sorry, the phone lines seem to be out.' Wendy was ripping the covering off a crêpe bandage. 'I'll try again later.'

Margaret signalled to Jennifer as she stepped into the hallway. 'Edith's got a nasty avulsion,' she said. 'And the skin flap's all scrunched up and torn.'

'Put a moist dressing on it,' Jennifer directed. 'I'll come and sort it out in a few minutes.' She moved quickly towards the door further down the hallway as the surgery bell sounded again. Jennifer paused for a second, not wanting to enter the maternity suite until she was able to focus completely on her patient. Her level of tension needed lowering.

If the phones were out there was no way of ringing home, but Saskia was far more responsible than most girls her age. If there had been any problem getting all the children home safely, she would have found some way to contact Jennifer on her mobile. She could reach Brian on his own cellphone if absolutely necessary but calling him in to help deal with a stressful influx of casualties was the last thing Jennifer wanted to do. Wendy and Margaret were both very capable nurses. Surely even this storm couldn't throw anything at them more than the three medical staff could deal with. There was nothing life-threatening about the injuries arriving so far and as long as Liz's labour was straightforward, they should be fine. Jennifer took a deep breath and entered the maternity suite.

'Sorry to have been gone so long, Liz,' she told her patient cheerfully. 'Let's have a look at you and see what's happening.'

Ten minutes later, Jennifer headed back to the treatment room. Wendy and Margaret now had Edith on the bed.

'I've had a go at straightening this flap.' Wendy looked up, the tweezers poised in her gloved hand. 'What do you think?'

Jennifer eyed the wound. 'Couldn't have done better myself. Could you dress that, please, Margaret?' She waited until Wendy had dropped her gloves into the rubbish bin near the door. 'Liz is about six centimetres dilated so she's definitely in labour. I've set up the Entonox for her to use for pain relief but it's better if she keeps moving at the moment. Can you stay with her?'

'Sure.' Wendy nodded. 'Sam McIntosh is in the consulting room with his mother. He needs looking at.'

'What happened?'

'Apparently the wind caught the garage door and it hit him on the head. Possibly unconscious but only very briefly. He seemed fine but rather quiet. Jill got worried when he vomited about half an hour ago. Looks like concussion.'

Jennifer knew Sam well. Six years old, he was the same age as the twins. Sam lived just down the valley from Jennifer's property and often came to play after school. He looked pale and unusually subdued at present.

'I'm going to shine a bright light in your eyes,' Jennifer told the small boy. 'Try and keep them open for me.'

She managed to complete a full neurological check and reassure Sam's mother before another interruption occurred. This time it was her cellphone. The flash of panic that something had happened at home intensified when the caller identified himself as Robert Manson, one of the local fire officers.

'We've got an accident near Barry's Bay.' Robert's voice was difficult to hear over the crackle of static and the background noise of the weather and people shouting. 'We need you on scene, Jennifer.'

'How bad is it?' Barry's Bay was well away from the route the children would have taken and they had probably been home for hours by now.

'We've got one of the drivers trapped. He's unconscious. He's the worst but we've got a couple more patients.'

'I'm on my way.' Jennifer moved fast. She was donning over-trousers and her oilskin parka by the time Wendy found her.

'What's happened?'

'Car accident. We're going to need some help, Wendy. Do any of the other nursing staff have cellphones?'

'Not that I know of.'

'Get hold of Tom Bartlett, then, if you can. Let him know what the situation is.' If he wasn't already on the accident scene, their local police officer should be able to use his four-wheel-drive vehicle to round up some extra staff.

'Do you want Brian called back?'

'Not yet.' Jennifer was determined to keep her partner as a last resort. She picked up the large tackle box that contained her resuscitation kit. 'We need a bed made up for Sam. I want to keep an eye on him overnight. Run a neu-rological check every twenty minutes or so for now.' She gave her nurse an anxious glance. 'I hope I won't be too long.'

'Don't worry. We'll hold the fort,' Wendy assured her confidently. 'Rather you than me out in that lot. It's not going to be pleasant.'

Pleasant was an adjective almost as far re-moved as possible from anything that could de-scribe the conditions Jennifer found herself in. It was now only 5.30 p.m. but it felt like the middle of the night. The wind was strong enough to rock the solid four-by-four vehicle she was driving and the rain heavy enough to virtually obliterate visibility, even with the windscreen wipers on full speed. Waves crashed against the sea wall as she crawled slowly along the foreshore on the far side of the road. The force of the sea was enough to send a river of foamy water across the tarmac. Jennifer tried to dampen her alarm but her thoughts tumbled wildly.

She could imagine a newspaper headline. LOCAL DOCTOR WASHED OUT TO SEA IN STORM. What would the article say? 'Thirty-two-year-old Dr Jennifer Tremaine is missing, presumed drowned, having been swept from the road by a fatal combination of a southerly storm and a high tide.'

Jennifer changed gears as she reached the first hill past the township. The water level was well below her now but her imagination had been caught by the notion of the article. 'Dr Tremaine had been practising in her home town of Akaroa for nearly six years and was well used to attending emergency call-outs in any type of weather.' That would be true enough. They could even go to town on some of the more dramatic rescues she had been involved in. Like that one on the fishing trawler right out in the headwaters of the harbour. They could probably find the photographs that had been published on the front page of the newspaper a few years back, where the bus full of tourists had gone over the bank thanks to the snowdrifts which had obscured the side of the road. Jennifer had had her share of drama over the years but she had never encountered weather quite this vicious.

Her progress was slowed even more as she passed Duvauchelle by the hail that clogged the windscreen wipers and bounced off the bonnet of the vehicle. She smiled wryly. 'Dr Tremaine had never intended to practise medicine in a small rural hospital,' she invented aloud. 'After a highly commendable record at medical school, she had every intention of moving overseas. She planned to become a specialist surgeon, attached to a world-renowned unit— probably in the United States—and become famous for her incredibly brilliant skills and the unparalleled depth of knowledge in her field.'

Jennifer snorted and abandoned the mental game. She could see the flashing lights of the rescue vehicles ahead of her as the hail changed to sleet. She was about to get very wet and very cold, working under miserable conditions to save a life that could well belong to someone that she had known since childhood. The battles she fought were often personal and victory gave a level of satisfaction she would never had found anywhere else. Certainly not in the States and probably not even as a specialist surgeon. The fates that had delivered her home were probably a lot wiser than she had been. This was where she belonged and exactly where she was needed.

Robert Manson was directing a small but dedicated team of volunteers. They were using heavy cutting equipment on a badly crumpled car jammed against the bank. Another car was further up the hill, its windscreen broken and one side badly dented. The doors hung open and Jennifer could see a woman sitting sideways on the front passenger seat, her head cradled in her hands. Another person, presumably the woman's companion, stood motionless beside her, watching the activity down the hill. Jennifer left her own vehicle's engine running, with the heater on a high setting and the headlights helping to illuminate the rescue scene. She pulled her resuscitation kit from the back and joined the group of men between the fire engine and the car.

'Hi, Jenny!' Robert had to shout over the noise of the cutting gear. 'Sorry to drag you out in this. We shouldn't be much longer.'

'What's the patient's condition?'

'Still not conscious but he's got a good pulse and he's breathing OK. There's a doctor in there, stabilising his neck. We're just putting a neck collar on him.'

'A doctor?' Jennifer was taken aback, her position as the first medic on scene removed. 'Not Brian, is it?'

Robert shook his head. 'Don't know who he is. *Said* he was a doctor and he seems to know what he's doing. He arrived a few minutes after we did. He's got a camper van.'

Jennifer's gaze followed the direction of Robert's arm. The rain had eased to a steady downpour and she could see the shadowy outline of the large van in the intermittent glow of the flashing rescue lights. Someone on holiday, then. Jennifer would need some reassurance of their qualifications but if they checked out she would be only too glad to accept some assistance.

'Has anyone checked the other victims?'

'Not properly.' Robert looked back towards the second vehicle. 'Damn. I told them to stay inside the car, out of the rain. That chap's not even wearing a coat. He'll be frozen.'

'Get them into my truck,' Jennifer suggested. 'The heater's on.' She stepped back as the noise of the cutting equipment slowed and the fire officers pulled the mangled car door clear.

'We're ready for the backboard,' someone shouted. 'And the oxygen.'

Jennifer moved forward. The wind caught her hood, pushing it back and driving heavy rain into her face. She pushed her fringe back from her eyes, able to see the accident victim clearly for the first time. A young man, his face was injured and bloody but not enough to disguise his features. Jennifer felt a familiar twist of her gut. She knew the patient. He was Liam Bellamy—the son of the fisherman who had just had the hook removed from his hand.

'Liam?' Jennifer leaned closer and raised her voice. 'Liam? It's Jenny Tremaine. Open your eyes for me.'

'He's not responsive.' The deep male voice came from the back seat of the car. 'Except to painful stimuli. I'd put his GCS at about 8.'

'Airway clear?'

'It is now.'

Jennifer nodded. Liam's mouth was closed around the end of the plastic oropharyngeal airway.

'Here's the oxygen.' A mask was passed in beside Jennifer. 'It's running on 15 litres.'

Jennifer fitted the mask to Liam's face. As she pulled the elastic strap behind his head her hands brushed the arms of the man still supporting Liam's head. She glanced up, registering the stranger's appearance for the first time. She blinked and stared, her jaw dropping. The man smiled without amusement.

'Hello, Jennifer. Fancy meeting you here.'

'Andrew!' The name came out as an astonished gasp.

'Here's the backboard.' Robert's voice was right beside Jennifer's ear. 'How do you want to do this, Doc?'

'Slide the end of the board onto the seat. I'll look after his head and you take the legs. Let's keep him as straight as possible.' Jennifer nodded at the man in the back seat as he let go of Liam's head. She supported the weight on her shoulder, her arms around the young man's body as they turned and lifted their patient onto the backboard. The other members of the local rescue team crowded in to help lift the board onto the waiting stretcher and transfer it to the back of the modified Land Rover that served as an ambulance. Jennifer had her kit open and IV equipment already out by the time she was joined by her unexpected colleague. She didn't glance up until she had inserted the IV cannula and flicked the tourniquet open again.

'Andrew Stephenson,' she said softly. 'I just don't believe this.' Her gaze shifted. 'Is that saline ready to go, Mickey?'

The young fire officer nodded. He handed the end of the tubing to Jennifer who connected it to the line in Liam's forearm. She checked the flow as the bag was suspended, then reached for her penlight torch.

'Have you got a spare dressing?' Andrew was still standing outside the back of the vehicle. 'I've managed to cut my leg on some metal.'

Jennifer nodded. 'Find one for him, Mickey.' She was still focussed on her patient. She pulled Liam's eyelids open and shone the torch on his pupils. 'Liam, can you hear me?'

The response was an incoherent mumble of words but Liam's arms moved. Jennifer caught the one with the IV line in.

'Try and keep still, Liam,' she said firmly. 'You've been in a car accident.'

'He's lightening up a bit.' Andrew took a package from Mickey. 'Thanks, mate.'

'Why don't you get in out of the rain?' Jennifer suggested. 'I'll have a look at your leg.'

'I'm all right.' Andrew had his foot on the first step of the Land Rover. He enlarged the rip on the leg of his jeans.

'That's one hell of a cut.' Mickey sounded impressed. 'I think you'd better let the doc take a look.'

Andrew had already folded a large gauze pad and pressed it to his leg as Jennifer looked up. 'Andrew *is* a doctor, Mickey. We went through medical school together.'

Not precisely *together*, she amended silently, fitting her stethoscope to her ears. More like at the same time. Competing fiercely for the top spot of their intake. Alternating their positions at the head of the class and taking intense satisfaction in proving themselves superior to the other in whatever field they were competing. Academic, practical or even social—the struggle had blurred the boundaries of all aspects of those years. Looking back, the antagonism had provided a memorable background to Jennifer's tertiary education. It had been a fight she had revelled in. And the enemy had been Andrew Stephenson.

'You sound like an American tourist,' Mickey told Andrew.

'I've been living in the States for a few years,' Andrew responded. His tone was weary. 'I suppose I've picked up a bit of an accent.'

'Liam's got a flail chest but breath sounds are equal at present.' Jennifer's attention shifted briefly to Andrew. 'You're a general surgeon, aren't you?'

'Not any more.'

'What?' Jennifer's brow furrowed. 'Have you specialised in something, then?'

'Not exactly.' Jennifer's stare at Andrew wasn't productive. His head was bent, his attention on the dressing he was holding to his calf. A dressing that was already soaked with blood.

'Is that an arterial bleed?' Jennifer snapped.

A figure appeared beside Andrew before he had time to respond. Tom Bartlett glanced at Andrew's leg, then towards Jennifer.

'I've got one of the boys to take your truck back to the hospital with the two people from the other vehicle, Jenny. They don't seem to be injured badly but they'll need checking. How's Liam?'

'He's pretty seriously injured. Under normal circumstances I'd be calling for a helicopter to get him to Christchurch. We'll have to get an ambulance in by road.'

'No go, sorry.' Tom's face was grim. 'There's been a massive slip on the other side of the hilltop. Our access is completely cut off.'

Jennifer marshalled her thoughts rapidly. 'You'll have to come with me,' she told Andrew. 'I'm going to need some help.'

'I can't.' Andrew shook his head. 'I'm on holiday. My camper van's over there.'

'I don't give a damn about your holiday.' Jennifer couldn't believe Andrew's casual attitude to this situation. 'This is serious,' she told him coldly. 'Liam's *life* might depend on you sacrificing a few hours of your precious leisure time.'

'What I meant was, I don't have a current practising certificate for New Zealand.' Andrew met her furious glare without blinking. 'I'm not licensed to treat patients here.'

'I don't give a damn about that either,' Jennifer said briskly. 'You're qualified to help. And you need medical attention yourself. You've already lost quite enough blood.'

'What about the camper van?'

'Stop arguing and get in,' Jennifer ordered. She looked at Tom. 'Can you sort out the van?'

'Sure. Where do you want it?'

'The hospital car park is blocked. Have it taken up to my place.'

'Hang on a minute—'

Jennifer ignored Andrew's protest. 'Did Wendy get hold of you, Tom?'

'About extra staff? Yes.' Tom nodded confirmation. 'I got hold of Janey and she's going to round up Michelle and Suzanne.'

'Great.' Jennifer's head swivelled. 'Let's get going, then, Mickey.'

The fire officer climbed down the steps and looked at Andrew. 'You'd better get in,' he told him, 'so I can fold these steps up and shut the doors.'

Andrew paused for another moment, shaking his head in disbelief. Then he climbed into the back of the vehicle, sitting heavily on the bench seat that ran parallel to the stretcher.

'I knew this holiday was going to be a disaster,' he informed Jennifer. 'I've known it for nearly a year.'

'Why did you come, then?' Jennifer was fitting the electrodes from the lifepack to Liam's chest and a pulse oximeter to his finger. Her tone was unsympathetic.

'I couldn't miss it.' Andrew gave a snort of laughter that held no amusement. 'After all, it *is* my honeymoon.'

CHAPTER TWO

IT WAS not a moment to offer congratulations. Jennifer Tremaine ignored Andrew Stephenson's statement regarding his holiday and the odd implications it carried. Jennifer didn't care about the reasons Andrew had returned to this side of the globe or why the trip might be proving less than satisfactory. If there was a new wife sulking in the back of the camper van because of some marital dispute, Tom could sort it out. Andrew certainly didn't seem bothered but that was hardly surprising to Jennifer, given what she remembered about the man. She could put aside what she thought of his personality, however. The fact was, he was here, and Jennifer badly needed the professional skills he was capable of providing. When Mickey slammed the back doors of the Land Rover closed she almost smiled with satisfaction. She had Andrew Stephenson trapped for the moment and she was taking him in the direction she had chosen.

Despite the protective wet-weather clothing, Jennifer was soaked and cold. She took a moment away from her assessment of Liam Bellamy's condition to reach for some towels in an overhead locker. The thick, dark blonde curls of her hair were plastered to her head and still dripping enough water to be a real nuisance.

'Blood pressure's 100 over 60,' she informed Andrew as she roughly dried her face and hands. 'Heart rate's up to 130. He's shocked, but his airway's still clear and his breathing hasn't deteriorated any further.' She shoved a fresh towel towards her passenger. 'Get yourself a bit drier,' she ordered. 'You must be frozen. Wrap yourself in a blanket as well.'

'Thanks.' Andrew took the towel with one hand. His other hand was still holding the dressing on his lower leg. The thick gauze wadding was saturated and a trickle of blood moved through the fingers holding the pad in place.

'Put some pressure on that,' Jennifer directed.

'Thanks.' Andrew's tone was much less appreciative this time. 'But I do remember the basics of haemorrhage control.'

'Try to implement them effectively, then,' Jennifer suggested. She turned back to Liam, her stethoscope in her ears again. The gap in time since she had last had any contact with Andrew Stephenson seemed to have evaporated effortlessly. A casual snipe at each other and they were back to communicating the way they always had. Time clearly hadn't changed Andrew, but Jennifer was faintly ashamed that she could slip so easily into what she considered an immature and less than professional mode of interaction. She rose quickly, bracing herself against the stretcher as she pulled open another locker. She took out a bandage and one of the largest sterile dressings available, ripping open the packages as she turned back.

'Fold this up,' she directed Andrew, handing him the large gauze wadding. 'I'll put a pressure bandage on and maybe that will stop the bleeding.' She tried to smile at Andrew as he looked up—a form of apology for her lapse in courtesy—but he didn't return the gesture. As Jennifer stooped and began to bind the bulky dressing firmly to his leg, he picked up the towel and dried his face. Jennifer worked rapidly, taking only seconds to finish her task. It was long enough to gain a physical impression of the man, however. The muscle beneath her hands felt like iron. Andrew hadn't gained an ounce of flab over the years. If anything, he was even leaner than he had been.

'That saline's almost run through. You'd better start another unit.'

'OK.' Jennifer reacted promptly. Perhaps Andrew was taking more notice of Liam's condition than the impression he had given. Maybe he would be more inclined to offer his assistance when they had some better facilities available. *If* they ever got back to the hospital. Mickey seemed to have brought the Land Rover to a complete halt.

'What's going on, Mickey?'

'I'm watching the waves,' Mickey called back. 'The wash is right over the road just here and I don't want us stuck in the middle if we catch a big one.'

At least they were only minutes away from the hospital. They only had to head up the hill a little way and turn onto Napoleon Drive. There was a tense silence in the vehicle as they waited. Jennifer listened to the roar of the surf as it covered the sound of more hail on the roof above them. They moved with a jerk as Mickey accelerated to clear the patch of road between waves. Jennifer leaned closer to Liam.

'We're almost there,' she told him. 'Don't worry, Liam. We'll soon have you sorted out.'

Her patient moved convulsively, coughing and then retching. He was gagging on the plastic airway and the oxygen mask filled up with blood. Jennifer uttered a dismayed oath as she wrenched it clear of his face before he could inhale any of the contents. The airway tube fell to the floor and rolled beneath the stretcher.

'Get him on his side,' Andrew ordered crisply.

Jennifer was already doing her best but Liam was a well-built young man and hardly moved when she grasped his shoulders to pull him over. Suddenly it seemed as if Liam was rolling himself onto his side and Jennifer realised that Andrew was beside her, lifting and turning the heavy body with apparent ease.

'Have you got a suction kit?'

'On the wall behind you. There's a clip underneath.' Jennifer was holding Liam's head, keeping his airway open. She hoped the rough manoeuvre hadn't exacerbated any injury. 'I hope he doesn't have a pelvic fracture.'

'I'd say his airway and breathing are more of a priority right now,' Andrew responded coolly. 'Here...' He handed her the tube from the suction kit and switched the unit to full power.

'You do it,' Jennifer told him. 'I need to find another OP airway and a bag mask.'

'I'm not wearing gloves.'

'Then put some on.' Jennifer snatched the tube and cleared the blood from Liam's mouth and nose. She noted the cut inside his lip, the broken teeth and the probable broken nose, but were they enough to explain the amount of blood in the mask?

'I'll find another airway for you.' Andrew reached into the kit to extract one of the plastic devices. The abrupt halt of the Land Rover caused him to overreach.

'There's a bloody great tree blocking the driveway,' Mickey shouted. 'I nearly hit the damned thing.'

'Sorry.' Jennifer braced herself as the vehicle began reversing. 'I should have warned you about that. We'll have to go around the back by the kitchens.'

Andrew handed her the airway. He rapidly assembled the bag mask components and Jennifer plugged the tubing into the oxygen supply before fitting it over Liam's mouth and nose. She glanced at Andrew.

'GCS is dropping again. He's lost his gag reflex and his breathing is getting worse. He's going to need intubation as soon as we get him inside.'

'He needs evacuation to the nearest major hospital. You can't possibly have the facilities to deal with a patient in this condition here.'

'We'll have to,' Jennifer said tersely. 'We're the only chance he's got. There's no hope of evacuation in this weather.' She sent Andrew a warning glance. 'And I'm including you in that ''we''.'

Andrew shook his head. 'I told you—I'm no longer a doctor. I gave up medicine nearly a year ago.'

'Why?'

'That's my business.'

The Land Rover had stopped moving again. The engine idled and Jennifer could hear rain on the vehicle's roof in the silence that followed Andrew's cool comment. She squeezed the bag she was holding again, turning her astonished stare back to her patient. 'I don't care what your reasons were,' she announced. 'And you don't stop being a doctor just because you chucked your job in. Right now I need to assess and stabilise my patient. I need help and I'm going to use whatever resources I can find. Including you.'

The back doors opened and Jennifer moved swiftly, unhooking the end of the stretcher. 'Bring the lifepack and the suction kit,' she ordered Andrew. 'And follow us.'

Wendy and Margaret were both waiting by the open door as Mickey and Jennifer raised the stretcher and wheeled it towards the back entrance of the hospital.

'Tom Bartlett rang us,' Wendy informed Jennifer in a rush. 'Janey and Michelle are here, looking after the other patients. Sue's coming in as soon as she's dropped off her children. The treatment room's clear.' Wendy took a quick breath. 'How's Liam doing?'

'Not great.' It was Andrew who spoke as they moved past Wendy. 'Sats are dropping fast. Probably a tension pneumothorax from the rib injuries.'

Jennifer let Margaret take her place pulling the stretcher. 'I'll get a chest-drain kit set up,' she said, moving rapidly ahead and shedding her oilskin parka as she moved. The astonished stare directed at Andrew by both Margaret and Wendy had not been lost on Jennifer but she couldn't afford to be distracted by introductions just yet. Within seconds they were all crowded into the treatment room. Mickey, Margaret and Wendy positioned themselves around the backboard as Andrew held the head end and directed the transfer of their patient to the bed.

'On my count,' he instructed. 'One, two…three!' Andrew reached for Jennifer's stethoscope which had been left draped across Liam's abdomen. He glanced up as he lifted the earpieces clear a short time later. 'We're going to need a drain on both sides,' he informed Jennifer. His gaze raked Wendy. 'You're a nurse?' he queried tersely. 'I need some gloves.'

Jennifer could feel Wendy's hesitation. She gave her nurse a reassuring glance as she reached for a second sterile chest drain package. 'It's OK, Wendy,' she said calmly. 'Andrew's a doctor. A surgeon. He knows what he's doing.'

The tension in the room wasn't limited to the nurses' wariness of the strange doctor. The situation was critical and both Andrew and Jennifer worked in a tense silence as they dealt with Liam's respiratory collapse.

'Got it!'

Jennifer had heard the characteristic hiss of air escaping from the side of the chest Andrew was working on. She concentrated grimly on inserting her own drain, dimly aware of a familiar frustration at Andrew achieving a successful result first. It lasted only seconds.

'Haemothorax on this side.' Jennifer attached the drain to the bottle that Margaret had prepared. She watched the flow of released blood. 'Rather a large one.'

'A single rib fracture can cause a loss of 150 mls into the pleural cavity.' Andrew was picking up the stethoscope again. 'And this lad's fractured a fair few.' He nodded as he shifted the disc on Liam's chest. 'We've got equal breath sounds.' He glanced at Mickey who was ventilating Liam with the bag mask, then he looked at Jennifer. 'Are you going to intubate? Have you got mechanical ventilation available?'

'I'll do it now.' Jennifer was pleased to see that Wendy was already setting out the intubation kit. She stripped off her soiled gloves and reached for a new pair.

'What about X-ray facilities?' Andrew queried. 'We need chest, C-spine and pelvis.'

'No X-rays, sorry.'

'Blood pressure's dropping.' Margaret sounded worried. 'Ninety over fifty.'

Andrew's attention flicked to Margaret. 'Get the rest of his clothes cut off,' he directed. 'I'll check his abdomen and pelvis. You get on and do the intubation, Jennifer.'

Margaret's hesitation was only momentary. Jennifer could sense her rapid acceptance of directions from someone who was clearly in control of the situation. Turning to pick up the laryngoscope, she caught Wendy's gaze. Her nurse was clearly questioning Jennifer's apparent acceptance of being cast into the role of an assistant by someone who was, after all, a complete stranger despite the demonstration he was giving of his obvious abilities. Jennifer merely nodded at Wendy and Mickey, who had stayed to assist.

'We'll get the collar off and you can provide manual in-line stabilisation for us, Mickey. You can do the cricoid pressure when I'm ready, Wendy. This may not be easy with the facial injuries Liam has.'

Jennifer concentrated on her task of securing Liam's airway, confident that Andrew and

Margaret would be dealing with anything else that might need urgent attention. If Andrew's involvement came with the price of giving up leadership of this small team, Jennifer was quite willing to pay. This was no time to even remember old battles but Wendy wouldn't have questioned Andrew's take-over if she'd known him like Jennifer did. Andrew had never been able to resist taking command of any situation he found himself in—particularly one that included her own presence. Jennifer was more than happy to let this one go. She had a professional colleague whose skills matched—probably exceeded—her own, and Jennifer was grateful for the shared responsibility as she registered the comments she overheard from further down the table.

'Pelvis doesn't feel unstable,' Andrew was saying. 'Any femoral fractures?'

'Nothing obvious.'

'We need some more fluids. Find me a 12-gauge angiocath.' Andrew spoke to Margaret as though they were familiar colleagues. 'I'll go for the groin. He's completely shut down peripherally. Do another blood pressure, too, would you, please?'

'Sure.'

Jennifer had Liam's head positioned now and stable. 'Hyperventilate with the bag mask, Wendy. I'm ready to intubate.'

'Blood pressure's 80 on 55,' Margaret told Andrew.

Jennifer tried to concentrate on visualising the larynx and vocal cords. Part of her brain registered Margaret's comment with dismay. Liam was becoming progressively more shocked. He was losing more blood than could be accounted for by the injuries they had identified so far. If they were going to save Liam Bellamy's life they needed to find the source of the blood loss and control it. Until then they had to maintain an adequate circulation.

'We'll push saline into this larger line,' Andrew decided. 'Have you got haemaccel as well?'

Jennifer eased her laryngoscope into its final position. 'Pass me a 9-mm tube, thanks, Wendy, but don't release pressure on the cricoid cartilage just yet.'

Andrew had instigated the rapid fluid replacement by the time Jennifer had inflated the cuff on the endotracheal tube and set up the ventilator. He was eyeing the chest-drain bottle on her side of the bed.

'He could have a diaphragmatic rupture,' he suggested to Jennifer. 'It would explain a continued blood loss of that rate and a lack of abdominal distension if he's injured his spleen. Given the rib fractures on that side, it seems quite likely as a source of major blood loss.'

'Find another bottle, Margaret,' Jennifer requested. She looked at Andrew. 'What about a peritoneal lavage?'

'What about it?'

Jennifer suppressed a flash of annoyance. The reminder of how often she and Andrew had disagreed over a diagnosis or method of treatment again wiped out the gap in time very effectively. They had always challenged each other, demanding justification for opinions or decisions. Trying to prove themselves more capable than the other.

'It could be diagnostically useful.' Despite the inappropriate setting to dredge up old battle skills, Jennifer couldn't quite help the edge of sarcasm in her tone. 'If we got lavage fluid coming from the chest drain, then we'd know for sure that there was a diaphragmatic rupture.'

'And what then? Are you proposing a laparotomy if it's indicated?' Andrew's eyebrow was raised sceptically. 'Are you qualified to undertake a procedure like that?' He glanced around the treatment room. 'Here?'

'No, I'm not qualified,' Jennifer said quietly. 'But you are.'

'No, I'm not.'

Jennifer could feel the astonishment of both her nurses and Mickey. She ignored the rising tension. 'You're a specialist surgeon,' she reminded Andrew. 'The last I heard, you were so good you got poached from the Boston Memorial to join some very prestigious private outfit.'

'That's ancient history. I told you, I'm not practising any longer.' Andrew's tone suggested that either Jennifer's memory or her ability to understand were well below par.

'Why?' Jennifer was blunt. She wasn't about to let Andrew back out now. 'Did you kill somebody?'

Andrew's face darkened as his features froze for an instant. His eyes met Jennifer's directly. 'No.' His tone was as cold and calm as the stare she was receiving. 'And I'm not about to take the risk of doing precisely that by operating on someone in less than ideal circumstances.'

The alarm that sounded on the cardiac monitor was brief. The arrhythmia settled spontaneously after a few erratic heartbeats but it was enough to remind both doctors of their patient's still critical condition. The tap on the door of the treatment room came in the short silence that followed the cessation of the alarm. A young nurse aide poked her head around the door.

'Dr Tremaine? Could you come and check on Liz, please?' Michelle's face was anxious. 'She's in a lot of pain and the machine that's doing the baby's heart rate is beeping.'

Jennifer caught Andrew's dark eyes again with a silent plea. He transferred his gaze to Liam, his expression resigned.

'I'll do the lavage,' he said. 'And we'll take it from there.'

'Thanks.' Jennifer was suddenly aware of how pale and weary Andrew looked. Her own cold, damp clothing was clinging to her skin and Andrew must be a lot more uncomfortable than she was. He had been out in the storm far longer than she had and he was injured as well, yet he hadn't voiced a word of complaint.

'Tom Bartlett is here as well,' Michelle said to Jennifer. 'He wants to talk to the other people that were in the accident. Oh, and Mickey's wanted back at the station.'

'OK.' Jennifer stripped off her gloves. She couldn't afford to worry too much about Andrew Stephenson's level of comfort just yet. 'Wendy, you come with me. Margaret can stay and assist Andrew.' Jennifer paused as she followed Mickey to the door. 'Marg, find Andrew a set of scrubs when you get a minute. His clothes are soaked and he must be frozen.'

Wendy trotted behind Jennifer as they made their way towards the maternity suite. Jennifer grinned at her colleague.

'I wonder if Andrew might fancy doing a Caesarean?'

'Who *is* he, exactly?' Wendy's eyes were round. 'And where the hell did he appear from?'

'He's on holiday and was involved in the accident somehow.' Jennifer stopped beside a large cupboard. 'I'll get some dry scrubs for myself, I think.' She reached for a set of the pale blue theatre clothing.

'He's amazing,' Wendy continued in awed tones. 'And he's so... He's...' She gave a silent whistle.

'You wouldn't be the first woman to find Andrew Stephenson attractive,' Jennifer told her nurse wryly. 'And you won't be the last.' She was rapidly unbuttoning her shirt, screened by the open cupboard door.

'How do you know that?'

'I went through medical school with him.' Jennifer stripped off the damp shirt and replaced it with the loose, thick cotton top. Then she peeled off the oilskin over-trousers she was still wearing.

'Did you go *out* with him?'

'Heavens, no! I couldn't stand the man.' Jennifer pulled scrub trousers over her jeans for extra warmth. 'And he couldn't stand me either.' She shot Wendy a quick grin. 'I'm quite pleased to have him around right now, though.'

'You and me both. He's real knight-in-shining-armour stuff, isn't he?'

'Don't get your hopes up.' Jennifer felt obliged to issue the warning, having noted the gleam in Wendy's eye. She moved on briskly. 'You'd be wasting your time,' she added as Wendy caught up.

'Why?'

'He's on his honeymoon.' Jennifer didn't see Wendy's disappointed expression. She could see Tom waiting further down the hallway. 'I'll go and check Liz,' she told Wendy. 'You take Tom in to see those other patients. I think Janey might be with them. Find out whether she's got an update on young Sam as well. I want to know how he's getting on with that concussion.'

Elizabeth Bailey was miserable. 'That stuff isn't helping any more,' she told Jennifer, waving dismissively at the Entonox cylinder. 'My back is killing me.'

'I'll give you something stronger in a minute.' Jennifer was watching the foetal monitor as she pulled on clean gloves. The heart rate had dropped a fraction but not enough to be a problem yet. She would reset the level for the alarm as soon as she had examined Liz.

Suzanne Smith arrived just as Jennifer administered a dose of pethidine to her patient.

'Where do you need me most, Jen?'

'Right here.' Jennifer moved out of earshot to speak to the nurse. 'Liz is definitely in labour this time but things are moving very slowly and it's a classic ''backache'' labour. She's been here since this morning and she's still only six to seven centimetres dilated. She's had enough and we might have a long way to go till the end of stage one.' Jennifer shook her head. 'Goodness knows how we'll cope if the baby doesn't turn. Under normal circumstances I'd evacuate her. What's the weather like out there now?'

'Awful. And the road's still blocked. I heard it on the radio.' Suzanne bit her lip. 'I heard about Liam. How's he doing?'

'I'm about to find out.' Jennifer managed to smile at Suzanne. 'I'm so glad you're here, Sue. At least I know I've got Liz in the hands of a very capable midwife. I may be busy for quite a while.'

'I'll know if I have to call you. Best of luck.'

They were going to need more than luck. Liam Bellamy's condition had deteriorated further by the time Jennifer returned to the treatment room.

'He needs an urgent laparotomy,' Andrew declared. 'He also needs a blood transfusion. Have you got any frozen, fresh plasma?'

'No.' Jennifer eyed the second chest-drain bottle which was nearly full. 'Maybe we could do an autologous transfusion and reuse his own blood.'

'We'd need to anticoagulate the blood. I don't expect you'd have a cell-saver system available.'

'No. We've got plenty of anticoagulation agents, though.'

'Not much point pouring it back in unless the leak is fixed. My guess is a ruptured spleen. His liver could also be a likely candidate.'

'Could you repair it?'

Andrew shook his head slowly. 'You don't know what you're asking, Jennifer. We don't have the facilities or the staff. Not even an anaesthetist.'

'I can do an anaesthetic,' Jennifer offered promptly. 'It was my first rotation as a registrar. We've got the gear. The instruments are even sterilised on a regular basis. They used to do quite a bit of surgery here in the old days. And my nurses are great. Wendy and Margaret could both help.'

Andrew was still shaking his head. Jennifer caught hold of his arm. 'I took a fish hook out of a man's hand earlier today,' she told him with quiet intensity. 'He put himself in considerable danger trying to make sure his boat was going to be safe in this storm. His fishing boat is his living and the only way he can support his family. He's desperate to hold things together since his wife died three years ago. His kids are all he has. Liam is his eldest son.'

Jennifer could feel the muscles in Andrew's arm tense beneath her hand. She fixed her eyes on his face, willing him to agree. He still looked pale. The skin stretched across the strong lines of his features and deep lines around his dark eyes suggested that he was in pain…or unwell. Jennifer swallowed quickly. Was *that* the reason he'd given up his career? He'd just lost a significant amount of blood himself from the leg injury. He'd been exposed to the elements and put under stress. Had that exacerbated some underlying serious medical condition?

'Are you all right?' Jennifer queried urgently. 'Are you *able* to operate?' She almost reached up to touch his face. Her concern for Andrew's state of health wasn't purely for Liam's sake. Andrew Stephenson needed medical attention that only she would be able to provide. She was in a position of crisis here and somebody had to lose at least in the short term. The question was, who could afford to wait?

'I'm able.' Andrew's response fell into the tense silence. Jennifer felt her breath being released in a sigh of relief and unconsciously tightened her grip on Andrew's arm with a grateful squeeze.

Andrew nodded down towards Jennifer's upturned, eager face. 'I'm able,' he repeated with more emphasis. His solemn expression softened as his mouth twisted into a lopsided smile. 'And I'm willing.' The smile faded. 'We'll need a small miracle if we're going to be successful, you realise.'

'Miracles happen.' Jennifer tugged Andrew's arm gently as she turned him back towards their patient. 'Sometimes they just need a bit of a push to get them started.'

CHAPTER THREE

'I STILL can't believe it.' Jennifer's hazel eyes were alight with triumph. 'We *did* it!'

'He's not out of the woods yet.'

'He's relatively stable. He's come through the surgery and the bleeding is controlled. His blood pressure's up and he's breathing well on ventilation.' Jennifer was smiling as she leaned over a tray and selected a suture needle. Andrew's eyelids drifted slowly closed again but Jennifer didn't notice. 'They've almost cleared that slip on the road and there's a team coming from Christchurch to transfer Liam to the intensive care unit. They'll be here within a couple of hours.'

'He still needs blood.' It seemed to be a major effort to open his eyes again. Andrew had never felt so tired in his entire life. Even the strain of nearly three hours of conducting major surgery under primitive conditions wasn't

64

enough to explain this weariness. 'I'm O-negative,' he informed Jennifer.

'Mmm.' The light above the couch in the consulting room was catching Jennifer's bent head. Her hair had dried during its confinement under the cap she had worn in their makeshift operating theatre. Now Andrew could see it was still the colour he remembered so well. A rich honey blonde. And it was still just as curly, with soft waves that almost reached her shoulders. 'Can you feel this at all?' Jennifer asked.

'No. You put in enough local to numb an elephant.'

'I needed to. This cut was right down to the bone. It must have hurt like hell.' Jennifer was concentrating on her task. Andrew watched in fascination as she caught the tip of her tongue between her teeth for a second. He could feel the tug deep in his calf muscle as another stitch was knotted into place. 'No wonder you bled like a stuck pig,' Jennifer commented.

'I'm O-negative,' Andrew repeated.

'So you said.' Jennifer glanced up. Her lips twitched as she reached for scissors. 'I have to admit I couldn't spot that. It looked just like ordinary blood to me.'

Andrew snorted. 'You're missing the point, Dr Tremaine. O-negative is a universal donor.'

'Are you suggesting I've forgotten everything we learned at med school?' Jennifer sounded cool. 'I might point out that my marks in biochemistry were often better than yours.'

Andrew sighed inwardly. Jennifer hadn't changed a bit. She still assumed that anything he said was in some way a criticism of her. She was still far too quick to defend herself by going into verbal attack mode. 'What I'm suggesting is that I could donate some blood to young Liam Bellamy. A bit more haemoglobin circulating would do him a lot of good right now.'

'You look like you could use a bit more yourself.' Jennifer dropped the curved needle into a tray and picked up another. 'We're up to skin level now,' she told Andrew. 'I'll try not to leave you with too much of a scar.' She frowned at her patient. 'You're still looking rather pale. I think you probably lost more blood than I realised. I certainly wouldn't even consider taking any more.' Jennifer bent her head to her task again. 'Besides,' she added casually, 'who knows what sort of condition your blood is in?'

'What's that supposed to mean?' Andrew forced his weariness a little further away.

'I'm talking about infectious diseases,' Jennifer responded calmly. 'Things like hepatitis or HIV.'

'I wouldn't have been licensed as a surgeon if I posed any threat of transmitting disease.'

'How would *they* know?'

'Try regular blood tests.' Andrew felt a flush of annoyance. 'I've been vaccinated for hepatitis and have documented proof that I'm clear of HIV.'

'And when was your last test? Before or after you gave up your position as a surgeon?'

Andrew pushed aside the blanket covering his body. He felt distinctly overheated now. 'Does it matter?' he snapped. 'Are you really interested in my sex life?'

'No. Of course not.' Andrew could see a faint flush of colour staining Jennifer's cheeks.

'Good. Because I would have nothing of interest to tell you. My sex life would bore anyone. Including me.'

Andrew felt a trickle of perspiration on his face. Was the heat responsible for giving him this wave of dizziness and nausea? Or was the stress of the last few hours catching up? Jennifer hadn't been wrong about that cut hurting like hell. The pain hadn't gone until she'd pumped local anaesthetic into his leg. And he *had* lost a lot of blood. He'd pushed himself to the limit after agreeing to operate on Liam Bellamy. While the assistance he'd had had exceeded expectations, it had still been a major achievement on his part to remove Liam's spleen and control the massive abdominal blood loss. He was beginning to feel distinctly spaced out now. He gave up the effort of keeping his eyes open.

'My sex life is non-existent,' he heard himself saying. 'How's *that* for boring?'

The silence was odd. Andrew wondered whether he'd actually said the words aloud. Surely not! He opened his eyes to find Jennifer staring at him. Her expression was more peculiar than the silence.

'You said you were on your honeymoon.'

'I am.' A silly grin plucked at the corners of Andrew's mouth.

'So where's your wife?' Jennifer was still staring. Lord, her eyes were gorgeous. Huge and round with the shade of hazel an exact match for the darker tones in her hair. Andrew blinked.

'I didn't bring her,' he told Jennifer cheerfully. What was wrong with him? He was actually enjoying confessing his failure. 'I'm starting a new trend,' he added. 'Solo honeymoons.'

'Are you feeling all right?' Jennifer was standing up. She appeared to be swaying slightly. 'You look a bit hot.'

'It *is* hot. This place is like an oven.'

'It is warmer than it was,' Jennifer conceded. 'Jimmy came in to stoke up the old boiler because the emergency generator doesn't cover the central heating. I'm not hot, though. I think I'll take your temperature.'

'Who's Jimmy?'

'Our caretaker. He's married to Ruby.'

'Who's Ruby?'

'Our cook.' Jennifer was rummaging in a drawer. 'Where *is* that thermometer?' She glanced over her shoulder at Andrew. 'Ruby came in as well. She's making sandwiches for everybody. Are you hungry?'

'No. Have you finished with my leg?'

'I just need to put a dressing on it.' Jennifer abandoned her search for the thermometer. She picked up a sterile pad and a crêpe bandage instead. The knock at the door of the consulting room halted her return to Andrew's side.

'Hi, Tom. Come in. I'm nearly finished here.'

Tom nodded at Andrew. 'I just dropped by to let Mr Stephenson here know that his camper van's been delivered to your place.'

'Thanks, Tom. How are things looking out there?'

'We're over the worst. The weather's starting to clear and there's been no more accidents reported. The kids are all fine, by the way. Saskia wanted to know when you'll get home.'

'Not for a while yet, I'm afraid.'

Tom nodded again. 'I'll let her know. Is there anything you need here?'

'We're fine,' Jennifer told the police officer. 'Thanks to Andrew here, we've managed to cope with a fairly large crisis.'

'So I heard.' The glance Andrew received was one of respect. 'John Bellamy's here. Margaret's taken him in to sit with Liam. He'd like a word.'

'Of course. Tell him I'll be there in a minute.' Jennifer turned quickly back to Andrew as Tom left the room. She peeled the backing off the clear, sticky dressing. Now it was Andrew's turn to stare at Jennifer.

'Kids?' he queried softly. 'How many have you got?'

Jennifer was beginning to wind the crêpe bandage around his leg. 'Let's see.' She smiled. 'There's Angus. He's three. The twins, Jess and Sophie, are six and Michael's the oldest at eight.' She glanced up with a quick grin. 'I suppose I'd better count Vanessa as well. She's still a baby at six months old.' Jennifer reached for a roll of tape.

Andrew was stunned. *Five* children? And the oldest was eight years old? His weary brain didn't want to do the calculations. His chest felt tight. No wonder he'd never stood a chance. Jennifer must have been pregnant for the first time before she'd even married Hamish. Well before she'd left medical school. No wonder she'd given up her ambitions to be a surgeon herself. It was amazing she found time even to be a country GP.

'There.' Jennifer smoothed the tape holding the bandage in place and stripped off the gloves she was wearing. 'Why don't you have a rest while I go and check on Liam? Ruby's getting your clothes dry so you'll be able to get out of those scrubs soon. I'll get her to bring you a cup of tea.'

Andrew wasn't listening. So many questions were forming themselves in his fuzzy brain. Like why wasn't Jennifer wearing a wedding ring? And where was Hamish? Surely the man voted most likely to succeed in their year hadn't lowered his sights to a career in a small, rural hospital? But if he wasn't around, how come Jennifer was still producing babies? And how could she possibly still look as young and attractive as ever when she was the mother of *five*? The tightness in his chest changed to a tickle and then a major irritation.

'That's a nasty cough.' Jennifer frowned. 'Are you sure you're feeling all right?'

'I'm fine.' Andrew forced himself to a sitting position. 'I had a viral illness a couple of weeks ago. Left me with a touch of bronchitis.'

Jennifer was still frowning. She fiddled with the end of her stethoscope. 'Maybe I should give you a proper check-up.'

'Forget it. You've got real patients to see to. Like Liam.'

'Wendy's quite capable of monitoring things. She'll come and get us if we're needed.'

The second knock on the door made them both expect an instant summons to Liam, who still lay in the treatment room, but it was Suzanne who appeared in the doorway.

'We need you, Jen. Liz has been in second stage labour for over an hour. The baby hasn't turned and I'm not happy. Liz is exhausted and the foetal heart rate is dropping slightly during contractions.'

Wendy's face appeared beside Suzanne's. 'Liam's ECG is showing a few irregularities,' she informed Jennifer. 'Can you come?'

Andrew watched as Jennifer straightened her back. He could see the determination to cope in her face as it settled into a look of grim focus. She must be as tired as he was. She'd worked a full day before being called out to that accident site and she'd coped brilliantly with the unusual stress of major surgery being conducted in her treatment room. It must be years since she'd worked as an anaesthetist and it hadn't been easy, dealing with a patient in Liam's critical condition. She had two patients needing urgent attention now and he suspected that others were waiting. That middle-aged couple from the accident for starters. He swung his legs over the edge of the couch. His loose scrub-suit trousers unfolded to cover the bandage on his leg.

'You see to the baby,' he told Jennifer. 'I'll look after Liam.'

Gratitude for Andrew's unexpected offer of assistance stayed with Jennifer until she stepped into the maternity suite. Then everything else was forgotten. Elizabeth looked awful. Her face was puffy and her eyes swollen and red. A considerable number of tears had clearly been shed since Jennifer had last seen her patient. She picked up the damp cloth lying on the bedside locker and sponged her patient's face gently as she absorbed her impression of the young woman's condition and watched the trace of the foetal monitor.

'You've been coping so well, Liz. You're not having an easy time of it, are you?'

The response was a strangled sob. Liz was lying on her side, curled up as much as possible. She turned and failed in her attempt to smile at Jennifer. 'I've been trying so hard,' she said miserably. 'But I'm so tired now and the pain in my back is getting worse and worse.' Liz sniffed loudly. 'I'm just glad Peter's not here. I never want to see him again. This is all his fault.' She sniffed noisily again. 'I've decided I don't want a baby any more. Can't you make it just go away?'

Jennifer squeezed her hand before reaching for the face mask that lay abandoned beside the pillow. 'Have a few good breaths of Entonox and then see if you can lie on your back for me. I need to see what this baby of yours is up to.'

Jennifer felt her patient's abdomen carefully before donning gloves for an internal examination. 'You're fully dilated, Liz, and the baby's well down in your pelvis, but there's a wee way to go yet. Are you still getting strong urges to push?'

Liz groaned. 'I can't push any more. It hurts so much and I'm just too tired. I'm sorry, Jen,' she sobbed. 'I feel like such a failure.'

'You're not a failure at all,' Jennifer said firmly. 'I know you wanted to manage this by yourself, love, but I think you've tried hard for long enough. It's time we did something about helping this baby out now.'

Liz nodded but her eyes were fearful. 'What are you going to do?'

'I'm going to help the baby out with some forceps.'

'Will it hurt?'

'I'm going to give you some local anaesthetic. This should be a simple and quick procedure and I suspect it will be a lot less painful than these contractions you're having right now.'

'Let's get it over with, then.' The effort to smile was more successful this time. 'Please?'

Jennifer returned the smile before catching the midwife's relieved glance. 'I'll need some Kielland forceps, Sue. And draw up 20 mls of one per cent lignocaine. I'll get scrubbed.'

Suzanne joined Jennifer at the basin a minute later. 'Do you want me to catheterise Liz?'

Jennifer shook her head. She had soaped her hands and was reaching for the scrubbing brush. An opened sterile pack lay nearby, containing a gown, gloves and towel. 'A urinary catheter is good to avoid urethral bruising if it's likely to be a difficult delivery, but it's better to minimise the risk of introducing infection to the bladder if we can and I think we'll get away without one this time.' Jennifer picked up the towel to dry her hands. 'This should be straightforward. Liz is fully dilated, the head's engaged and there's no obstruction to delivery. The real indication for a forceps delivery here is that Liz is too exhausted to make any further effort herself and we're starting to see signs of foetal distress.'

'We're all set, then.' Suzanne tied the strings at the back of Jennifer's gown.

The procedure was as straightforward as Jennifer had hoped. By the time the pudendal block had taken effect, the local anaesthetic had removed even the severe back pain Liz had been suffering. The specialised Kielland forceps were eased into position and Jennifer exhaled a soft breath of relief as she gently rotated the baby's head from a posterior to an anterior position. With the contraction Liz supplied immediately afterwards, it was only seconds until the baby was delivered. Suzanne was ready with a soft suction tube and then Jennifer lifted the crying infant onto her mother's abdomen. Liz already had her hands outstretched to touch her baby for the first time.

'It's a girl, Liz, and she looks just beautiful.'

'One-minute Apgar score of ten,' Suzanne reported with satisfaction.

Jennifer was clamping the umbilical cord. 'The delivery of the placenta shouldn't take long, Liz. You'll get a few more contractions but you may not even feel them. How's the pain now?'

'What pain?' Liz was crying again but smiling through her tears. 'Oh, why isn't Peter here? Isn't she gorgeous?'

'You're not even going to need any stitches,' Jennifer informed Liz. 'Which is just as well after all this little one's put you through.'

'Have you decided on a name?' Suzanne was leaning over the baby.

'I've thought of a lot of new ones in the last few hours.' Liz grinned. 'None of them were very complimentary. Maybe we should call her Storm.'

'The storm's over now.' Jennifer was basking in the peaceful elation that followed a successful birth. Especially a difficult one. But there was more to her response than professional satisfaction. There was the sheer miracle of watching the introduction of a new life and the deep stirring within her own body that was an unmistakable yearning for a baby of her own. Maybe one day.

'Don't go all clucky on us.' Suzanne was watching Jennifer as she softly touched the baby's cheek. 'We can't afford to have two doctors out of action.'

Jennifer wasn't altogether surprised that Suzanne had caught up with news of Brian Wallace's angina attack. The community was a small one and the group of hospital employees a tight band within that community. News travelled fast amongst people with a genuine concern for the well-being of those closest to them.

'Fat chance of that,' she responded lightly. 'As if I'd have the time. Or the opportunity.'

'I don't know about that. What's this I hear about our visiting surgeon being an old boyfriend of yours?'

That did surprise Jennifer. When had Suzanne had the chance to get filled in on Andrew's history? The staff had probably had a good gossip while she had been closeted in the consulting room with the man, stitching up that nasty gash on his leg. The story had obviously been embellished along the way. Jennifer would have thought the night had provided more than enough excitement without some fictional account of her love life at medical school.

'He was never a boyfriend,' she denied emphatically. 'Merely an acquaintance.'

'A good-looking one,' Suzanne said with a grin. 'And what's he doing here if he wasn't planning to visit you?'

'He's on his honeymoon.'

'Oh! That's a shame.' Liz had been following the exchange between the doctor and midwife with considerable interest as she cuddled her baby.

'Where's his wife, then?' Suzanne asked suspiciously. 'I hear she wasn't in the camper van.'

'He hasn't got one.'

'Yes, he has. Tom said he parked it at your place.'

'I'm talking about a wife, not a camper van.'

'How can you have a honeymoon without a wife?'

'I've got no idea.' Jennifer was annoyed by the resurgence of her own curiosity regarding Andrew's absentee wife. She concentrated on examining the placenta, which had been expelled without Liz even noticing. 'Why don't you ask Mr Stephenson about that?'

'I couldn't do that. Far too personal a question.' Suzanne threw Jennifer a meaningful glance.

'Neither could I,' Jennifer said firmly. 'I haven't even seen the man for nearly eight years, for heaven's sake. For all I know it's wife number three that's done a runner.'

'Yeah, sure.' Suzanne's expression implied that a woman running from Andrew Stephenson was an unlikely scenario. And she'd only had a brief glimpse of the stranger. Jennifer sighed. At least the placenta was intact and she could be happy that the delivery was now completely over. 'I'll leave Sue to get you tidied up, Liz. I'd better go and see what else needs doing.' Jennifer straightened and stretched her back, walking towards the window as she stripped off her gown and gloves. 'Do you know, I think the rain has stopped? Even the wind is dying down.'

Finding that Liam's condition was again stable and being effectively monitored by Andrew, Jennifer finally managed to relieve the nurse aide who had been caring for the other accident victims. Michelle met Jennifer outside their room.

'I don't think there's much wrong with them,' she reported. 'Mr Hessler has a sore arm and Mrs Hessler is crying a lot, but she doesn't speak much English.'

It took Jennifer only a few minutes to reassure herself that the Hesslers hadn't suffered any serious injuries. Although there was no obvious fracture to Mr Hessler's arm, Jennifer splinted the painful limb and made arrangements to have him taken to Christchurch the following morning for an X-ray. She left Michelle to settle the couple for the night.

The responsibility for Liam's care was being transferred by the time Jennifer had completed a quick check on the other inpatients they now had. Sam McIntosh wasn't showing any signs of serious damage from his head injury and

Edith Turner was resting comfortably with her leg elevated. Mrs Dobson and Lester had both slept through the unusual level of activity in the small hospital. John Bellamy was most in need of Jennifer's attention and as much reassurance as she felt she could honestly give. He travelled with the emergency evacuation team from Christchurch as they transferred his son to Intensive Care by ambulance. As the vehicle pulled away, Jennifer checked her watch to find it was nearly one a.m.

'Go home and get some sleep,' Margaret told her firmly. 'Everything's under control here and Suzanne and Michelle are both going to stay till morning. We'll get things cleaned up.'

'I'll stay, too, if you like,' Wendy offered.

'No, you go home,' Jennifer told her. 'I'll need you again in the morning.'

'I could certainly use some sleep,' Wendy admitted. 'What a night!'

Jennifer smiled at the staff assembled in the hospital kitchen. She was too tired to help make any inroads into the vast pile of sandwiches Ruby had left for them. 'You've all been wonderful,' she told her nurses and aides. 'Thank you. I couldn't have coped without you all.'

'It could have been a lot worse,' Wendy commented quietly. 'We were lucky to have Andrew Stephenson to help.'

'Where is Andrew?' Jennifer asked. 'Has he had anything to eat or drink?'

'He said he wasn't hungry,' Michelle responded.

'I think he's getting changed,' Margaret added. 'Ruby put all his clothes through the drier.'

Jennifer left the kitchen as the other women prepared to go home or attend to duties. Suzanne was taking some sandwiches and a pot of tea to Liz. Michelle went with Margaret to begin the clean-up required in the treatment room after the surgery. Jennifer made her way down the now quiet and darkened hallway, looking for Andrew. She needed to thank him and find him somewhere to sleep for the rest of the night.

The light in the office made his whereabouts easy to discover. Jennifer tapped on the half-open door in case he hadn't finished dressing. Hearing no response, she entered the room. The scrub suit lay neatly folded on her desk. Andrew was tucking his shirt into jeans. He pulled them closed hurriedly but seemed to have difficulty with the fastening.

'I can't find my shoes,' he told Jennifer.

'They may not be dry yet.' Jennifer couldn't help watching Andrew fumbling with the snap fastening. The difficulty was being caused by the fact his hands were shaking.

'M-my sweater's m-missing, t-too.'

Jennifer stared. Andrew was shivering violently enough to stammer and yet he was looking flushed. He clearly wasn't well and she remembered the coughing spell he'd had earlier. Jennifer pulled the stethoscope from around her neck.

'Don't do those shirt buttons up,' she directed Andrew. 'I want to listen to your chest. Sit down for a minute.'

'I'm fine.'

Jennifer gave a fairly pithy response to refute Andrew's claim and she had the disc of her stethoscope on the front of his chest before he could object further.

'Haven't you had enough doctoring for one night?' Andrew asked irritably.

'Be quiet,' Jennifer commanded. She moved around Andrew to listen to his back. Then she felt his forehead before grasping his wrist to take a pulse rate.

'I thought so,' she said grimly. 'You're sick, Andrew. You've got a double pneumonia. You've got a tachycardia of 130 and you're hot enough to fry eggs. I'm going to admit you and start some IV antibiotics.'

'Like hell you are. I've had quite enough of this place, thanks. I'm going home.'

'And where is home, precisely?'

Andrew glared at Jennifer. 'Wherever I want to make it. I want to get back to my camper van.'

'You're not leaving here until you've got antibiotics on board.' Jennifer was thinking fast. The camper van was on her property. Surely he wouldn't be crazy enough to try and drive somewhere else in his current condition. She would at least be able to check on him in the morning and enforce further medical treatment if his condition was any worse. 'You need a course of tablets—enough to last at least ten days. Also, you'll have to give me your keys until I've checked you over tomorrow.'

'You can't do that.'

'Yes, I can,' Jennifer said smugly. 'Your van's parked at my house. How do you think you're going to get there?'

'I'll call a taxi.'

'We don't have taxis here.' Jennifer gave Andrew a very direct look. 'I'm going to find your shoes and sweater and a large syringe. If you don't want IV treatment then you're going to start with a loading intramuscular dose somewhere a lot more painful.' Her smile twisted with something very close to amusement. 'Don't bother doing your jeans up. I'll be back very soon.'

Andrew looked mutinous as he sat hunched on the passenger seat of her four-by-four fifteen minutes later.

'A loading dose of tablets would have been quite sufficient,' he muttered.

'Not in my opinion,' Jennifer told him airily. 'And if you're not considerably better in the morning, you'll be getting another injection.' She cast a sideways glance at her passenger. 'What you really need is a set of chest X-rays and a full blood screen.'

'It's only bronchitis.'

'Yeah, right!' Jennifer concentrated on the road as she negotiated still flooded patches. At least the tide had turned and waves were no longer breaking on the road. The rain had diminished to a light drizzle and visibility was good even as she left the streetlights and turned up a valley into the hills, following the road to Long Bay.

Andrew was silent for long enough to make Jennifer look at him with concern. His eyes were shut and a noticeable sheen of perspiration gleamed on his forehead. She should have insisted on leaving him in the hospital overnight. A camper van was no place for someone as sick as Andrew to sleep.

The rattle as they crossed the wooden bridge over a wide stream made Andrew's eyes flicker open. 'Where the hell are we?' he demanded.

'My ancestral estate,' Jennifer replied. The tree-lined driveway wound its way up another hill. 'It was part of a large farm when I was a child but most of it has been sold off now. We've got about twenty acres left but a lot of that is native bush.'

The house was large and square. An old weatherboard structure with two stories and wide verandahs on both levels. A barn stood at right angles to the house and a series of stable doors closed off half the side facing the driveway. The open area at the end of the stalls was lined with bales of hay and long wall hooks that supported farm equipment and tack. Jennifer's usual parking spot under the shelter of the loft was occupied by the camper van.

'You'll have to give me the keys.'

'No way.' Jennifer climbed out of the vehicle. The front door of the house opened beside them and a young woman in a dressing-gown hurried down the verandah steps.

'How am I supposed to get inside, then?' Andrew sounded exhausted rather than angry as Jennifer opened the passenger door.

'I'll unlock the van for you.' Jennifer's head turned. 'Hi, Saskia. Everything all right here?'

'Fine, apart from a few tree branches down. The kids are all sound asleep. I waited up for you.' Saskia was staring openly at Andrew who was hanging onto the car door as he stood up.

'This is Andrew Stephenson,' Jennifer told Saskia. The girl nodded.

'Doug told me about him when the van got dropped off.' Saskia was still staring.

Having finally hauled himself to his feet, Andrew swayed for a few seconds before lurching towards Jennifer. She caught him, supporting his body as she pulled his arm over her shoulders. 'Andrew's not feeling very well,' she said unnecessarily. 'Can you take his other arm, Sass? We need to get him inside and into a bed.'

Andrew mumbled something about the camper van and his keys. Jennifer ignored him as she and the teenage girl struggled to manoeuvre the heavy man towards the house and up the steps.

'Where shall we put him?' Saskia queried. 'On the couch? Or shall I move one of the children?'

'I'd rather not disturb anyone,' Jennifer decided, 'but the couch is no good. I'm going to be up looking after Andrew in any case. He can go in my bed.'

'Yeah.' Andrew's speech was much clearer this time. 'Just what I always dreamed about, Jen.'

'Yeah, right.' Jennifer grinned at Saskia's widened eyes. 'Don't pay any attention to him,' she advised. 'He's a sick man.'

'Not that sick,' Andrew declared. 'It's true, Jen. I've always—' He broke off as he began to cough. The spasms were clearly painful and Andrew was drenched in sweat by the time they reached the bedroom. As the women let go, Andrew collapsed onto the double bed. His breathing was rapid and laboured.

'I'll get him undressed,' Jennifer said. 'Could you get my kit from the back of the car, please, Saskia? Bring that portable oxygen cylinder as well if you can manage it.' She pulled Andrew's shoes off as she spoke. 'I have a feeling this is going to be a long night.'

Andrew's eyes opened again briefly. He even smiled at Jennifer. 'The longer the better,' he murmured. 'Come to bed with me, Jen. I want you.'

'You'll regret saying that tomorrow,' Jennifer assured him. 'If you even remember it, that is.'

His eyes closed and he turned his head with feverish distraction. She eyed the male figure that was now firmly ensconced on her own bed, the dark head indenting her pillows.

'I might regret this as well by tomorrow,' she muttered to herself. 'And I'll certainly remember it.'

CHAPTER FOUR

IT HAD to be a dream but Andrew was in no hurry to wake up.

The usual types of frustration were there. Limbs not responding to commands to move. Speech trapped inside his head or slurred incomprehensibly around a tongue that felt swollen and dry. An exhaustion that swept him repeatedly and inexorably towards periods of sweet oblivion. Yet Andrew knew who was providing the touch of those cool hands. He could focus instantly on the soft, gentle tones of her voice even if he couldn't quite force his eyes open. He could feel intense gratitude at the comfort her hands brought or the relief of drops of fluid in his parched mouth even if he was unable to express it. And when he could open his eyes he recognised the woman that had haunted his dreams seemingly for ever.

There were other people in his dream as well. Most of them were short and bouncy and were often being told to be quiet. A taller girl with a ring in her nose had weird hair like sheep's wool that was an improbable shade of purple, and there was a fat baby who got pulled around on a bright red tray with wheels. The stuff of dreams, all right. There were even dogs that appeared with startling regularity, like the hairy black one that leapt into view whenever that peculiar weight on his legs was removed. Andrew didn't mind any of this. He drifted, enjoying the dream that seemed to have the potential to descend into nightmare at any time but never quite tipped over the edge.

Somewhere along the line his eyes began to focus more clearly. He could see the tiny gold flecks in the hazel depths of Jennifer's eyes as she bent close, her stethoscope pressing firmly on his chest. He could appreciate the elegance of her hands, the long, tapered fingers holding a thermometer with a delicate touch. Fingers with neatly manicured nails but unadorned with any polish—or rings. Why wasn't she wearing any rings?

The short people gathered names that stuck. Michael and Jess and Sophie and Angus.

Angus was inclined to make fire-engine noises. Vanessa was the fat baby in the red trolley and it was Michael that usually provided the propulsion. The girl with the weird hair was Saskia and all these people seemed to smile a lot. Like Jennifer did. Had he forgotten the way her lips curved so deliciously to reveal small, perfect teeth? Or the tiny dimples that formed at the corners of her mouth halfway into the wide smile? Perhaps he had forced it out of his memory because of the effect it had. Her smile had never been just for him. Except now, by some strange twist of fate, it was.

'You're looking a lot better.' Jennifer was, indeed, smiling as she turned off the thermometer. 'Your temperature's down for the first time and your chest sounds a lot clearer. How are you feeling?'

'Great.' The word came out as a peculiar croak and Andrew blinked. How long had it been since he had spoken out loud?

Jennifer was smiling again. 'I'll bet.' A line appeared between her eyes as she frowned. 'You've been pretty sick, Andrew.'

'Have I? I can't remember much of the last few hours, I must say.' Andrew's mouth felt as dry as a desert but his voice was returning. 'I've been asleep.'

'No, you've been delirious,' Jennifer informed him. 'And it hasn't been a few hours. Try a few days.'

'What?' Andrew tried to concentrate. He stared suspiciously at Jennifer. 'That's not true.'

'It is,' Jennifer contradicted. 'If you hadn't been so sick I would have shifted you into hospital. Instead, we filled you up with fluids and antibiotics and looked after you here. See?'

Andrew looked above his head. The high brass knob on the bedstead had a bag of IV fluid taped to it. A line snaked down to reach his arm.

'I can take this out now,' Jennifer decided aloud. 'We'll start you on oral antibiotics and I suspect you could probably manage a cold drink by yourself. Or maybe a cup of tea.' She deftly slid the cannula from his arm and pressed a swab to the puncture site.

'I am thirsty,' Andrew admitted. He yawned. 'I still feel very tired. Are you sure I'm not dreaming all this?'

'Quite sure. Do you not even remember us helping you to the bathroom?'

'No.' Andrew could feel a flush spreading up his neck. He tried to ignore the unpleasant prickle of embarrassment. 'Where am I, precisely?'

'In my house,' Jennifer said. Then her lips twitched with amusement. 'In my bed, if you want to be really precise.'

'Oh, hell!' The embarrassment intensified. 'This is awful.'

'That's not what you said the first night you got sick.' Jennifer grinned. 'But never mind. It's all water under the bridge now—like those trips to the bathroom.' She moved away from the bed. 'Be careful when you try standing up. You're going to be a bit wobbly for a while yet. There's a glass of water here but I've got time to get you a cup of tea before I go to work if you'd like one.'

'I think I'd like to go back to sleep.' Andrew wanted to get back to the dream. He hadn't been in anyone's home there, let alone their bed. And there had definitely been no trips to any bathrooms.

'That's a good idea. Saskia will be in to see you as soon as she gets the children off to school.'

Andrew didn't bother to ask who Saskia was. He had too much new information to assimilate already. It was too exhausting to try and worry about any of it. He closed his eyes and willed the dream to return. For a time, he thought it had. The girl with the purple hair was talking to him but he couldn't make out what she was saying. The tuning in was involuntary and must have been due to the tone demanding a response.

'So, how 'bout it, then?'

'What?' Andrew's voice had rusted up again. He tried to clear his throat. 'Sorry, but who are you?'

'I'm Saskia.' The nose with the ring through its side tilted up. 'I'm Jen's housekeeper.' Bright green eyes were challenging Andrew to question her position. 'And I look after all the kids.'

Andrew licked his dry lips. Surely she couldn't be real. 'I don't want to appear rude, Saskia,' he said slowly, 'but what happened to your hair?'

The girl grinned and suddenly seemed even younger. How old was she anyway? Sixteen? Far too young to be a housekeeper and Andrew didn't even want to think about Jennifer's enormous brood of children.

'Don't they have dreadlocks where you come from?'

'I guess they do.' Andrew found himself returning the smile. The girl's confidence was rather appealing. 'Not usually purple, though.'

'It's aubergine, actually.' Saskia's remarkable long, woolly locks bounced as she turned her head swiftly. 'Elvis, get *down*,' she said sternly.

Andrew almost laughed aloud. This place was better than a circus. Now the girl with the aubergine hair was about to introduce him to the ghost of Elvis Presley. He became aware that his legs were no longer pinned to the bed. A shaggy black shape materialised beside Saskia and sat wagging a plumed tail.

'Sorry. He keeps sneaking in here. He seems to like you.' Saskia's keen glance appeared to be prepared to give Andrew the benefit of any doubt and go along with the dog's opinion. 'Can I get you something to eat or drink?'

'Eat?' Andrew's dream had not included any notion of food.

'My cooking's not *that* bad,' Saskia confided. 'Especially if it comes out of a can. My best things are baked beans or soup.'

'Soup sounds good.' Andrew was feeling more awake now. He shifted his position slightly and became aware of the need to move further. 'Um…Saskia?'

'Yeah?' The green eyes were scrutinising him again.

'Where's the bathroom?'

'Right there.' Saskia point at the door behind her. 'It's just as well we put you in Jen's room, with the *en suite*. It hasn't been easy, getting you to walk.' She raised an eyebrow. 'Do you want me to help you get to the loo?'

'No,' Andrew said quickly. 'Thanks, but I think I can manage by myself now.'

'Good.' Saskia grinned again, acknowledging the visitor's embarrassment. 'There's a shower in there if you feel up to it, and Jen put a razor by the basin.' She was still smiling. 'Designer stubble's OK for movie stars but...'

Andrew was feeling his chin. If he'd needed any proof of the length of time he'd been out of it, the heavy growth of beard was more than enough. 'I must look dreadful,' he murmured.

'Yeah.' Saskia nodded solemnly. 'You're still really pale and your face is thin and that stubble really needs to go west.' She screwed her face into thoughtful lines. 'Still, I reckon you'll be quite good-looking when you've cleaned up a bit.'

'Thanks.' Andrew was really smiling now. It felt even rustier than his voice had. 'I'll see what I can do.'

Jennifer was astonished by the difference in Andrew's appearance when she arrived home early that evening. Being clean-shaven helped a lot but the faint flush of normal colour in his skin was a huge relief. She'd had serious doubts over the last few days about the wisdom of nursing Andrew at home but, Brian had backed the decision.

'In days gone by it was routine to nurse pneumonia patients at home. He's a young, fit man. You've got him on good antibiotic cover that we can modify if necessary once we get the results from the blood tests. You're keeping his fluids up and he's going to get more peace and quiet here than he would in a hospital ward.'

Jennifer hadn't been sure about any of it and her doubts were compounded by guilt. Was Andrew as fit and healthy as he should be? He was a few years older than she was, having entered medical school as a post-graduate student with a science degree already. He looked older than the thirty-six years he would be now, and he was much thinner than she remembered him being. Quite frankly, he looked totally run-down. No wonder his bronchitis or whatever he'd had had developed into a much more serious illness. Especially after standing around in foul weather to help with a road accident.

She had allowed him to remain in his soaked clothing for far too long, only giving him dry things to wear so that he could remain standing for hours longer. Not only standing but performing a major operation in what must have seemed like barbaric conditions to a specialist surgeon. On top of that, he'd been injured himself and had lost a significant amount of blood. Little wonder he was still so pale. And as for peace and quiet in her house, Jennifer was well aware that her domestic situation often resembled a circus. She and Saskia had had to work hard to keep the troops under firmer control around their invalid. The novelty of a visitor, especially a man, had been a tempting prospect.

As if aware of her scrutiny, Andrew's eyes opened. His gaze caught Jennifer's and they stared at each other in silence for a short time. Jennifer felt suddenly shy under the focussed gaze. Andrew was once again in command of his mental processes but his helplessness over the last few days had altered her perspective so much that he seemed a stranger. For once, Andrew had not been trying to take anything over or to prove himself superior in any way. His dependence on her wasn't something the Andrew she'd known would have contemplated. Maybe now he would assert himself enough for them to argue. At least that way Jennifer could find herself back on familiar ground. She could forget the peculiar satisfaction that caring for Andrew had generated and consider her debt of gratitude for his self-sacrifice in helping her paid in full. She could even dismiss the guilt that she had exacerbated his condition by bullying him into offering that help in the first place.

'Hi.' Jennifer spoke first. 'It's time you had your pills.'

'What time is it?'

'Three p.m.' Jennifer was unscrewing the lid of the container she held. 'I came home early. It's very quiet at the hospital this afternoon and I got called out last night so I thought I'd spend some time with the children. I'll probably get called out again later.'

The mention of the hospital had focussed Andrew's thoughts. 'How's the boy? Liam.'

'He's doing really well,' Jennifer said with satisfaction. 'He's still under sedation in Intensive Care and being ventilated, but they've taken one chest drain out so far. He needed a massive blood transfusion but he didn't need to be taken back to Theatre.' She hesitated. 'There's been a few questions asked about the surgery we did and who you are. His consultants would like a written report.'

'Of course. I should have written it at the time instead of just giving a verbal handover to the transfer team. It was unprofessional.'

'It wasn't exactly a routine situation. We were coping with a crisis and you were already sick.' Jennifer chewed her lip. 'I'm sorry if I pushed you too hard.'

'I survived.'

'Only just.'

Andrew snorted. 'Have you got some paper and a pen? I'll do that report for you now.'

'It can wait. I've filled them in as much as I could remember and the consultants are happy enough. Liam would have died if you hadn't operated and they're well aware of that.

It's just a formality for the records now. It will keep until you're feeling a bit better.'

'I'm feeling a lot better,' Andrew claimed. He tried to push himself into a more upright position to prove his point but the movement was difficult. Part of the problem was the black dog lying on top of his legs again. 'Hullo, Elvis.'

'Get off the bed, Elvis,' Jennifer ordered. The dog's tail thumped the duvet. The rest of the shaggy body remained immobile.

'He's all right where he is,' Andrew told her.

'He seems to have adopted you.' Jennifer held out two tablets and a glass of water. 'Here. Swallow these.'

Andrew complied. Jennifer's eyebrows rose. 'Aren't you going to ask me what you're taking?'

Andrew smiled. 'You've had plenty of opportunity to poison me. It might seem somewhat ungrateful to start mistrusting you now.' His gaze dropped, to be caught by the previously unnoticed entourage Jennifer had brought into the room with her. An enormous tabby cat was pushing itself between Jennifer's ankles, ignoring a small, black kitten that was leaping energetically at the white tip of her tail. Andrew grinned. This place wasn't a circus. More like a zoo. Jennifer also looked amused.

Jennifer nodded. 'The cat's called Tigger for obvious reasons and the kitten's currently known as Trouble for reasons which will, no doubt, become apparent. Have you eaten anything today?'

'I had some soup.'

'Out of a can?'

'I think so.' Andrew remembered Saskia's description of her cooking prowess and grinned. 'It tasted great.'

Jennifer nodded. 'Sass is cooking dinner tonight.' She paused and flicked Andrew a conspiratorial glance. 'I might make you an omelette.'

'I don't want to be a bother.' How ridiculous, Andrew thought. He'd obviously turned this household upside down for several days. It wasn't an imposition he would have dreamed of putting on anyone. Particularly Jennifer Tremaine. He had never expected to even meet this woman again. Why had he even come here in the first place? Ah, yes. Andrew sighed heavily. The honeymoon.

Jennifer misinterpreted the sigh. 'It's no bother,' she assured him. 'In fact, I'll probably have an omelette myself.'

Andrew wasn't really listening. 'Where's the camper van?' he demanded.

'In the stable. It's quite safe.'

'It was due back in Christchurch on the fifteenth. What's the date now?'

'The seventeenth. I'll ring the rental company for you and arrange to have it collected.'

'No, I'll drive it back tomorrow.'

'I don't think so.' Jennifer looked stern. 'You won't be going anywhere for a few days yet.'

Andrew was silent. She was probably right. His session in the bathroom today had been a shock. He had struggled to manage the basic tasks of personal care. He'd felt as weak as a kitten and had become alarmingly out of breath with minimal effort. His silence was enough to let Jennifer know she had won the battle for the moment. It was broken by the sound of a door slamming and the approach of rapid footsteps.

'Jen, Jen—guess what?' Two excited small girls burst into the bedroom. The short people were back and this time Andrew could see they weren't part of any dream. They were far too excited…and noisy.

'Shh!' Jennifer warned gently as she held out her arms. 'Mr Stephenson still isn't feeling that well.'

'His name's Drew,' the twins chorused. 'Sass told us.'

Jennifer was startled. She turned to Andrew. 'You don't want the children calling you that, do you?'

Andrew returned the glance calmly. 'Sounds fine to me.' He wanted to ask why the children called her by her name but Jennifer looked rather distracted.

Jennifer *was* distracted. Totally. She was only half listening to the girls' chatter about the day's excitement. She had never called Andrew 'Drew'. It had been a name reserved for his friends at medical school and Jennifer had never been invited to use the diminutive.

But, then, she'd never offered him the use of the abbreviation of her own name. Andrew had always called her Jennifer. Apart from the other night when she'd brought him home and he'd been completely out to lunch by then, judging by the other rubbish he'd been talking. Jennifer had had a fair bit of talking to do later in order to convince Saskia there had been nothing at all going on between them. Ever!

'It's going to be in it tomorrow,' Sophie was telling Jennifer. 'Can we get one in the morning before we go to school?'

'I want one for news,' Jess added.

'No, I do.'

'Perhaps you can share,' Jennifer suggested automatically, wondering what on earth the girls were, in fact, talking about.

'Can we have one each?' Jess asked. 'Please?'

'Um…' Jennifer's rescue came in the shape of the tall boy who entered the bedroom. He was pulling the red trolley, which contained two younger children this time. A short brown and white dog squeezed past the trolley and shot into the room. The tabby cat promptly but calmly leapt onto the bed and dived beneath the duvet. Andrew blinked and his face took on a vaguely incredulous expression.

'Hi, Mike.' Jennifer looked over the pleading faces of the girls. 'I suppose you want one as well?'

'One what?' The boy slid a quick glance at Andrew and then stared at his feet. The pause was enough for the twins to rescue Jennifer this time.

'A newspaper!' they shrieked happily. 'With our *picture* in it!'

'Oh, *that*.' Michael shrugged. 'The guy only wanted to take it because of Saskia's purple hair.'

'No, he didn't. He wanted all of us.' Sophie's lower lip jutted ominously.

'How many people are in the photograph?' Jennifer asked quickly. 'Was it the whole school?'

'No. Just us and Saskia.'

'We stopped by the hospital to say hello on the way home,' Jessica explained. 'But you'd already left. They were getting ready to chop up that tree that fell in the driveway and the man from the newspaper got us to sit on it to show how big it was.'

The toddler climbed out of the red trolley, leaving the fat baby wobbling precariously. 'There was a big truck,' he told Jennifer importantly. 'With a spoon.'

'It was a bulldozer, Angus,' Sophie corrected her brother. She lifted the baby with some difficulty. 'It came to clean up the tree.'

'Oh, good.' Jennifer took the baby from the small girl. She'd been trying to organise the tree's disposal for two days but there had been a queue in the urgent clean-ups required in the aftermath of the storm. 'So!' She jiggled the baby and smiled at the children. 'You're all going to have your picture in the paper. How exciting! We'll have to get an extra copy to send to your dad.'

Andrew's jaw dropped noticeably. So Dad didn't live here? It must have been a recent exit. The fat baby Jennifer was holding was Vanessa, wasn't it? The six-month-old? And the split must have been remarkably amicable. Jennifer looked even more pleased than the children at the prospect of sending such an interesting missive.

A faint shout from another region of the house caused the children to race for the door. The speed with which they exited the room amazed Andrew. The small dog skidded in his eagerness to catch up but Elvis hadn't twitched a muscle. Jennifer laughed.

'It's afternoon teatime,' she told Andrew. 'I just hope Saskia hasn't been baking today.' Her voice dropped to a confidential whisper. 'Saskia's biscuits are like small bricks.'

Andrew summoned a faint smile. 'You've got a lot of kids,' he said slowly.

'I know. But it wasn't exactly by choice.' Jennifer grinned before Andrew could query the odd statement. 'Still, I wouldn't part with any of them but I'm sure they're a bit tiring for you at the moment. Especially *en masse*. I'll try and keep the visits down for a day or two but I'm afraid you're proving a rather irresistible novelty.'

'I don't mind.' Andrew was surprised to find this was a true statement. 'I like them.'

Jennifer beamed. 'They're great kids,' she said proudly. 'I always wanted a big family but it was a bit of a surprise to get them so fast.'

'I'm sure it was,' Andrew agreed carefully. 'I'm amazed you got through your houseman and registrar years with a baby to look after.'

'Oh, I didn't have any of them then,' Jennifer said lightly.

Andrew wondered if the wave of confusion was due to his weakened physical state. 'I don't understand,' he confessed finally. 'Michael's eight, isn't he?'

'Nearly nine,' Jennifer confirmed. A smile of comprehension lit her features. 'You didn't think they were *my* kids, did you?'

'Of course I did,' Andrew said irritably. He didn't like the feeling of having been misled. 'Whose children are they, then?' he demanded.

'My sister's.' Jennifer wasn't about to go into detailed explanations. She didn't like the way Andrew was demanding information. He was clearly feeling much more like himself. Then she sighed. He could be forgiven for be-ing curious. 'Except for this one,' she added, jiggling the baby again. 'Vanessa is Saskia's daughter.'

'What?' Andrew was horrified. 'She's only a child herself.'

'She's seventeen,' Jennifer told him. 'I found her sitting on the beach when she was about four or five months pregnant. Her family had kicked her out and she's been living with us ever since.'

'And your sister? Where's she living?'

'She's not.' Jennifer looked away. 'She died over a year ago.'

Andrew stared at Jennifer's closed face. She didn't want to talk about it so he wasn't going to push. There *was* something else he really wanted to know, however.

'What about Hamish? Are you still married to him?'

'I never was.'

'But you were engaged. Right through medical school.'

Jennifer sighed heavily. 'It's a long story.' She shrugged. 'I need to go downstairs. It's time I helped the children with their homework and Vanessa here needs her bath.' She turned away. 'You should rest.'

Andrew waited until Jennifer had almost reached the door before he spoke quietly.

'Jen?'

She turned sharply. Andrew wasn't delirious now. And he hadn't called her Jennifer.

'I'd really like to hear your story.'

'It's my business,' she responded coolly. 'Just like it's your business why you've given up being a doctor.'

Andrew almost smiled. Was she paying him back for being uncooperative? Was this another 'anything you can do, I can do better' game? They'd played that one often enough in the past. Maybe he hadn't been blissfully engaged throughout their medical school careers but he'd paraded enough female companions to ensure that Jennifer had never realised how empty his love life had really been.

'I'll make you a deal,' he offered softly. 'We'll swap stories.' He caught his breath. Was Jennifer even interested in his recent past? She had opened the door now but hadn't moved her feet. The internal debate she was having was reflected in her face. Her eyes narrowed slightly.

'Just tell me one thing, Andrew. Where's your wife?'

'I haven't got one. I'm not married. I never was.'

'Then why did you say you were on your honeymoon?'

'It's a long story.' Andrew resisted the urge to smile triumphantly. 'And you need to go downstairs.'

'I'll be back.'

Andrew let his head sink back onto his pillows. Elvis stretched himself and sighed with heartfelt canine contentment. Tigger settled himself more comfortably against his chest and a deep rumbling purr started up. Andrew felt at one with both his guests.

Jennifer wasn't married to Hamish Ryder.

The children weren't hers.

And she was coming back.

Suddenly, Andrew couldn't think of anywhere else in the world that he would rather be right now.

CHAPTER FIVE

THE urgency had gone.

The aftermath of the crises the storm had brought could have left Jennifer feeling drained. Instead, she was curiously content. The shake-up her world had experienced was over and the pieces were settling into a familiar, if somewhat improved shape.

The hours of consultation time this afternoon had been very ordinary. She'd seen a toddler with an ear infection, old Mr Bates who had prostate problems and Mrs Scallion who needed to start medication to control her high blood pressure. Alice Hogan, an excited young farmer's wife from Pigeon Bay, came in to have her long-awaited pregnancy confirmed and Edith Turner's leg was healing as well as could be expected. The older woman now had torches placed strategically around her house so she wouldn't trip over anything in the event of another power cut. Sam McIntosh came in after school for a check-up and was showing no evidence of any repercussions from his head injury. Jennifer invited him to come and play with the twins the next day.

'It's Saturday, so you can come for lunch and stay as long as you like,' she told Sam. 'If this fine weather keeps up we might get Button's saddle out and give him some exercise.'

'Isn't it lovely to see some sun again?' Sam's mother, Jill, was picking up her son's coat and schoolbag. She glanced at Jennifer. 'Are you sure it's OK for Sam to come over tomorrow?'

'Of course.'

'I wouldn't want you to get overloaded with visitors, especially at mealtimes.'

'It won't make any difference at all,' Jennifer assured her.

'I saw that camper van going down the road yesterday. Has that Dr Stephenson gone home, then?'

'Not yet. The rental company sent someone to collect the van.'

'Oh.' Jill looked thoughtful. 'I guess he's stuck here for a while, then.'

'Not necessarily. He can always catch a bus. There's just not much point paying a hundred dollars a day for a van that's not being used.'

'No,' Jill agreed. She didn't appear to be in a hurry to leave. 'I heard he was pretty sick.'

'He was. It's going to take him a few days to get back on his feet.'

'I also hear he's an old friend of yours. From medical school.' Jill's gaze was suspiciously eager.

'That's right.' Jennifer's response was cautious. She knew the gathering of parents at child collection time after school provided ample opportunity for the exchange of news and gossip, but just how much information had Saskia been sharing? Or the children for that matter. At least Sam was keen to get home. He was tugging at his mother's hand.

'I guess you've got a lot of catching up to do.'

'Mmm.' Jennifer merely smiled.

'Come *on*, Mum. I'm hungry.'

'See you tomorrow, Sam.' Jennifer followed them out of the consulting room. She wanted to collect her inpatient files from the office and do a quick ward round. Jill McIntosh had no idea how correct her statement had been, she reflected. She and Andrew *did* have a lot of catching up to do. They had even made a deal to do just that but that had been two days ago and no opportunity had presented itself. Andrew was out of bed for short periods now but there always seemed to be children around. Especially the twins. The novelty of a captive audience was too good to pass up. Drew had to be shown the wonderful picture of them all in the newspaper—several times. He was required to listen to reading homework and to watch how clever Zippy the terrier cross was at fetching tennis balls.

Artistic creations in the form of get-well cards and presents were being delivered at a rate of knots. The after-school effort yesterday had involved cardboard boxes, glue, dried pasta shells and poster paint. Michael's lack of contribution had been more than made up for by Angus, and the time the adults could have had alone after dinner had been spent washing paint from both the three-year-old's hair and Zippy's wiry coat. By the time the children had all been in bed, Andrew had also been asleep and Jennifer had been loath to disturb him. He needed rest more than anything else at present.

Besides, the urgency had gone. Andrew hadn't seemed bothered by the fact he was stranded without his own transport. He had offered to move himself into the shearer's cottage where Jennifer had stored his belongings or into a motel, but Jennifer had informed him she was quite happy sharing the enormous bedroom the twins occupied. He was to stay right where he was until she was satisfied his condition was vastly improved.

'You're still my patient,' she told Andrew sternly. 'I'm not going to have my reputation as a doctor in this town shot down by you collapsing in the street. Or some motel.'

Andrew's acquiescence had been surprisingly forthcoming. 'Just for a day or two,' he agreed. 'I'll be back on my feet properly by then.'

'We'll see,' Jennifer promised. It was her professional duty to make sure that Andrew stayed around until he had recovered after all, both from his illness and his leg injury. She was quite sure it would take somewhat longer than just a day or two. And Jennifer was happy that she had the situation well under control.

Her inpatients in the hospital were also under control. Mrs Dobson had received a new supply of talking books from the mobile library service and was happy to sit listening for hours at a time. Lester's pain levels were becoming more tolerable and he was keen to get home to his family. Elizabeth Bailey was ready to go home as well. Jennifer's final duty for the day was discharging the young mother and her baby. She followed the proud parents out to the car park where they fussed over securing the infant car seat.

'Bye-bye, Brooke.' Jennifer blew a kiss towards the baby before smiling at Liz. 'Sue will be in to visit you for the next few days to see how you're coping at home. Call me if you're worried about anything, otherwise I'll see you at Brooke's six-week check-up.'

She waved them off with a smile. Jennifer hadn't been surprised that the baby's father, Peter, had hated the suggestion of Storm for his daughter's name. In today's sunshine it would have seemed even more inappropriate. The Baileys' car turned carefully onto the road past a familiar vehicle waiting to turn in. Jennifer watched Brian Wallace climb out of his car.

'You're back early, Brian. I thought they were going to run all sorts of tests on you in the cardiology department.'

'They did—very efficiently. X-ray, ECG, echo, exercise test and bloods. And a consultation. I was most impressed.'

'And? What did they say?'

'I'm on a semi-urgent waiting list for an angiogram. I might need a repeat angioplasty or possibly bypass grafting.' Brian scowled. 'I guess I failed my exercise test.'

'What was the result?' Jennifer walked beside Brian towards the front entrance of the hospital. 'How long did you walk for?'

The response was a deliberate mumble. Jennifer grinned. '*How* long?'

'Ninety seconds,' Brian growled.

'And why was it terminated?'

'Bit of chest tightness.'

'Any ST depression?'

'A bit.' Brian wasn't slowing down as he pulled the door open. 'I could murder a cup of tea. I wonder if Ruby's done any baking.'

'Don't try and change the subject, Brian. I'll be having a copy of the results sent to me anyway. How much ST depression did you get?'

'Four millimetres. Maybe five.'

Jennifer bit her lip. The test had been very positive, then. Blood supply to Brian's heart had diminished sharply with minimal exercise and he was getting angina at rest. 'You should be on an urgent list for a cardiac catheterisation.'

'They don't have too much of a waiting list. I should get an appointment within a few weeks. I'm not in any hurry to find out bad news.' Brian looked over his shoulder briefly. 'How's everything been here?'

'No problems.' Jennifer recognised that she had received as much information as she was going to get for the moment. 'That was Liz and Peter taking the baby home that you passed on the way in. Lester's doing well—we can probably discharge him in a day or two—and Mrs Dobson has received enough talking books to keep her happy for weeks. Nothing exciting at the clinic but I've started Mrs Scallion on a beta blocker.'

'Have the results come back on her fasting glucose levels?'

'No. I was going to ring the lab about that.'

'I'll do it.' Brian was heading for the kitchens. 'After my cup of tea. Ah, Ruby!' Brian smiled at the tiny woman in the large white apron. 'That's not one of your famous chocolate cakes by any chance, is it?'

'It is,' Ruby acknowledged proudly. 'But I'm not sure if you're allowed any on your diet, Dr Wallace.'

'There's some nice crackers in the pantry,' Jennifer suggested innocently. 'And plenty of cottage cheese in the fridge.'

'Go home,' Brian told his junior colleague. 'I refuse to be ordered around any more today. At least, not until I get home and Pat starts bossing me about. This is the one place I'm still in charge and I intend to make the most of it. Ruby, love, pour me a cup of tea and let me enjoy a small slice of that cake.'

Jennifer gave in gracefully. Brian had insisted on taking call tonight and she hadn't argued about that either. The new problems he was facing with his health were enough of a blow without her damaging his pride further by trying to edge him away from the front line of the career he loved so much. While Brian had been very impressed with the way Jennifer had handled the crises during the storm, the fact that he'd been considered unfit to participate had distressed him deeply. The older doctor was being forced to consider his future seriously right now, and while Jennifer could do her best to ease his professional workload she couldn't take over. Brian had been quite correct in his statement. He was the senior half of the partnership and he was still in charge.

Besides, Jennifer was looking forward to getting home. The day at work had been quiet and the early August weather had decided to pretend it was springtime. The sunshine and warmth of the day was fading rapidly now but it had been enough to spark anticipation of the pleasures of a New Zealand rural summer. Relaxing family times with the children. Picnics on the beach and lots of swimming. Lazy afternoons mucking about with the pony or floating toy boats down the stream. The sort of activities that had lived on in Jennifer's memory from her own happy childhood and ones she could now share again with her sister's children. Maybe this summer would be happy enough to heal the scars more effectively. Especially for Michael.

Andrew declared himself well enough to join the family for dinner that evening, and he did look a lot better. He was still very pale, however, and Jennifer noticed that he paused to catch his breath on the way down the stairs. He ate very little but Saskia glowed with pride when he praised the lasagne.

'It came out of the freezer,' Saskia admitted. 'But sometimes I still manage to burn it.'

During the after-dinner flurry of clearing up, finishing homework and getting the younger children ready for bed, Andrew took himself into the living room adjoining the kitchen. Moving slowly, he set and lit the open fire and then eased himself onto one of the comfortable old couches nearby.

'I'm sick of staying in bed,' he responded to Jennifer's suggestion that he needed rest. 'I'll sleep a lot better if I stay up for a bit.'

Angus didn't need to stay up any longer in order to sleep well. His thumb was in his mouth by the time Jennifer carried him upstairs and his eyes closed the instant his head touched the pillow. Jennifer kissed the tousled curls and tucked the teddy bear under the covers. She left the nightlight on and went to the bathroom to check on the twins' progress. Jennifer sighed heavily at the sight that greeted her.

Damp towels lay abandoned on the floor. Discarded clothing lay amidst puddles of water and plastic toys that had clearly been thrown from the bath. The girls had made no attempt to tidy up after themselves and had now absconded. Jennifer fished under the bubbles to retrieve the soggy bar of soap and then pulled the plug. More toys became visible as the water level receded, including a rag doll that had no business being in the bath. Jennifer shook her head and moved downstairs with the intention of rounding up Jessica and Sophie. They could clean up their own mess.

The intention was postponed the instant Jennifer entered the living room. The scene was one of domestic warmth. The blazing log fire had much to do with the atmosphere, as did the old but comfortable furniture. Saskia sat cross-legged in a huge, cracked leather armchair, about to give Vanessa a bottle of milk. Michael lay on his stomach in front of the fire, using the poker to bat a tennis ball towards Zippy. Jessica and Sophie, fresh from their bath and cutely attired in fluffy pyjamas, sat on either side of Andrew on a couch. Elvis lay with his head on Andrew's foot and Tigger was ensconced on his lap. Andrew was reading a picture book to the twins. Both girls had a stack of other books beside them, clearly ready to extend the session as long as possible. One look at the absorbed expressions on the children's faces as they gazed up at Andrew, and Jennifer forgot about sending them upstairs.

She quietly began clearing up the pile of paper and crayons left on the table, hoping that Michael might be enjoying the story as well. Maybe the novelty of hearing an adult male voice in the house might bring her nephew out of his shell just a little.

Michael appeared disinterested, however. He poked the fire and watched the resulting shower of sparks. An ember landed on the hearthrug and Jennifer swooped, picking up the glowing fragment and throwing it back into the fire before it could burn her fingers.

'Don't do that, please, Mike,' she told the boy quietly. 'It's dangerous.' Jennifer put the container of crayons on top of the mantelpiece just as Andrew finished the story.

'This one now, Drew.' Jessica slotted a book into his hands swiftly.

'No—this one.' Sophie had a larger book, the corner of which dug into Tigger as she tried to position it.

'Don't do that!' Jessica admonished. She tugged Drew's arm. 'Sophie's poking Tigger.'

'I can tell.' Andrew nodded. 'She's digging her claws into my knee so she doesn't fall off.'

'Tell her to stop,' Jessica commanded. 'Anyway, she got to choose *Little Bear* so it's my turn to choose.'

'No more stories.' Jennifer felt obliged to rescue Andrew. 'It's time you two were in bed.'

'Drew could read us a story in bed.'

'Not tonight,' Jennifer said firmly. 'Drew's tired. He's still getting better and he needs a rest.'

'Oh, but—'

'No buts. And I want the bathroom tidied up, too. It's a disaster area.'

Michael poked the fire again. The embers crackled and popped.

'Nearly bedtime, Mike,' Saskia warned.

'No, it's not,' Michael responded loudly. 'I'm nearly nine and I don't have to go to bed until eight o'clock. It's only the girls who have to go to bed now.' The poker dropped onto the hearth with a resounding clatter. 'It's stupid not having a TV,' he announced. 'Other kids all do. We don't even have a computer.'

'Come on, girls.' Jennifer was beckoning the twins. 'Upstairs.'

'I've got a computer,' Andrew said casually. 'Would you like to have a look at it, Mike?'

'No.'

'I need to get it out anyway.' Andrew ignored the ungracious response. 'I've got a report to write for Jennifer.'

'Can we see your computer?' Sophie asked eagerly.

'Tomorrow.' Jennifer answered for Andrew.

'Why have you got a computer?' Jessica queried. 'Where is it?'

'In one of my boxes.'

'Jennifer put your boxes in the cottage.' Jessica could see a new direction to try and stall their departure. 'We saw them. You've got an awful lot of stuff.'

'It's all my worldly goods,' Andrew informed her solemnly.

'What are worldly goods?'

'Stuff.' Andrew grinned.

'Did you live in the camper van? Haven't you got a house?'

'Not any more,' Andrew admitted.

'Where do you live, then?'

'Nowhere, I guess.'

'Yes, you do!' Sophie wasn't going to be left out of this fascinating conversation. 'You live with us.'

Saskia was grinning broadly. 'This is the place for waifs and strays all right. Look at me.'

'Am I a waif?' Jessica was determined not to be ushered from the room. Jennifer took hold of her hand.

'Upstairs!' she ordered.

Jessica gave in. ''Night, Drew,' she said reluctantly. 'See you in the morning.'

'Sure.'

''Night, Mikey,' the twins chorused. Michael ignored his sisters. He had wriggled closer to the couch and was fiddling with the long plume of the black dog's tail.

'Has your computer got games on it?'

'Indeed it has.'

Jennifer was pulling both twins away. 'Why don't you find a torch, Mike?' she suggested. 'You could show Drew where I stored his things. He won't know where the key to the cottage is.'

It took some time to supervise the restoration of the bathroom, tooth- and face-cleaning chores and the eventual settling of the twins into their beds. Jennifer wondered whether Michael's interest had been stimulated. Perhaps a computer was just what he needed right now. She could ask Drew about what sort might be best. *Drew.* Maybe it was the children's use of the name that now made Jennifer feel awkwardly formal using his full name. Or maybe it was because he'd been drawn into her unusual family over the last few days. A gathering point for waifs and strays wasn't so far off the mark really, but the idea of Andrew Stephenson fitting that category was ridiculous. Or had been, until he'd become too ill to care for himself. There was no disputing how well he did fit in. No longer a stranger but not like a visitor either. He was carving a niche in the household that felt disturbingly comfortable. Sophie had declared that Andrew lived with them. Funny how Jennifer hadn't felt any urge to correct the little girl's statement.

Returning to the living room, Jennifer found Andrew and Michael sitting at the table. A laptop computer was plugged in and they were both absorbed by what was on the screen.

'You can use the mouse to jump the ravine,' Andrew was saying. 'See? You've got to get the timing right, though, or you'll fall in and there are giant spiders out to get you down there.'

'Can I try?'

The smile on Michael's face was fleeting but it twisted something inside Jennifer. How long had it been since she'd seen him really happy? Catching Andrew's gaze, she realised that she wasn't alone in assessing Michael's state of mind. Andrew looked as hopeful as she felt that the boy's reserve might be showing a crack. The phone rang as Jennifer smiled her acknowledgement. When she returned a few moments later, her expression was surprised.

'It's for you, Saskia. A man—but he didn't say who it was.'

Saskia looked disconcerted. 'Who'd be ringing me up?'

'Maybe it's a modelling agency,' Andrew suggested. 'They saw your photo in the paper and fell in love with your hair.'

Saskia grinned at Andrew. 'I'll show you how to do dreadlocks if you want.' Uncurling her legs, the teenager lifted her now sleeping baby. Jennifer held out her arms.

'I'll take Vanessa. I'll put her to bed while you get the phone.'

Saskia was curled up in the armchair again when Jennifer returned. She was staring at the fire with an expression that made Jennifer pause.

'What's up, Sass?'

Andrew's glance in their direction was swift. His touch on Michael's shoulder was light. 'That thing's got batteries,' he told Michael. 'Let's unplug it and you can take it upstairs and do battle with the spiders for a bit longer before you turn your light out.'

'It's OK.' Michael stood up abruptly. 'I've had enough, anyway.'

''Night, Mike.' Jennifer's smile was a little distracted. 'Don't forget to clean your teeth.' She picked a couple of small logs from the basket and knelt on the rug beside the two sleeping dogs to add the wood to the fire. Andrew moved to resume his position on the couch. Elvis roused himself with an effort, slipped onto the couch beside Andrew and immediately lapsed back into unconsciousness with his black, shaggy head now on the man's lap.

'Watch out,' Jennifer warned. 'He dribbles sometimes.' She stayed where she was on the rug, turning back to the unusually silent teenager. 'Who was on the phone, Sass?'

'My dad.'

'Really?' Jennifer's eyes widened.

'He saw the photo in the newspaper.' Saskia sounded very subdued.

Jennifer leaned forward and touched Saskia's leg. 'Are you OK? Did he say something to upset you?'

Saskia shook her head. 'It was weird. He said he missed me. That he's been trying to find me ever since I left.'

'How long ago was that?' Andrew asked.

'Ages,' Saskia told him sadly.

'Almost a year,' Jennifer added. 'Saskia ran away from home when she found out she was pregnant. I found her sitting on the beach in the middle of the night and she's been here ever since.'

'And you didn't let her parents know she was safe?' Andrew sounded incredulous.

'Of course I did. I rang as soon as Sass gave me her number. I spoke to her stepmother, Donna.'

'She told Dad I was in Auckland, staying with friends,' Saskia said. 'That's where he's been trying to find me. He went to the police and everything.'

'Did you have problems with your stepmother, Sass?' Andrew asked gently.

'You could say that. When she found out I was pregnant it was the last straw. She said I was a slut and it was just as well Dad had had some decent kids since he'd married her. She said I'd always been in the way and the sooner he kicked me out, the better.'

'And he did?' Andrew was outraged. 'He told you to leave?'

'I didn't wait to give him the chance.' Saskia turned to Jennifer. 'He said he never knew I was pregnant. That he had a granddaughter. I think…' Saskia added slowly, 'I think he was crying.'

'Oh, Sass.' Jennifer looked ready to cry herself. 'That's so sad. I can't believe your stepmother could have been so cruel.'

'I can.'

Both Saskia and Jennifer turned to Andrew in astonishment. 'You don't know anything about Donna,' Jennifer said accusingly.

'But I know what can go on in step-families. The preference that can be given to children that aren't even half-siblings. How your life can be made absolute hell by being left out, taking the blame for things you didn't do, being made to feel unwanted and in the way. Like nothing you could do would ever fix things.' Andrew spoke softly. 'Like you really weren't worth anything at all as a person.'

Saskia was nodding, her mouth gaping in amazement. 'How do you know that? Did you have a stepmother?'

'Stepfather. With two boys who were older than me. He wanted my mother enough to take on the burden of an unwanted child. My mother wanted him enough to put all her efforts into his sons. By the time I left home I was convinced that nobody would ever think I was special. I was going to have to make it on my own. It's the loneliest feeling in the world.'

'I felt like just walking out into the sea,' Saskia confessed. 'I'm so glad Jen found me.'

'You were lucky,' Andrew agreed. 'And you deserve to be. I'm not surprised that your dad misses you.'

Jennifer was watching the embers as she listened. Her opinion of Andrew was attempting another disconcerting U-turn. He'd always come across as vaguely superior at medical school. Aloof from the group. They'd assumed he'd considered their company undesirable but had it really been a lack of confidence on his part? Had he wanted to belong but hadn't made an attempt to avoid the risk of being rejected?

'Donna's left,' Saskia informed her audience. 'Gone back to her ex-husband, and Dad's on his own again. He wants to see me.'

'How do you feel about that?'

'I'm not sure. Excited, I guess. I need some time to get used to the idea.' Saskia uncurled her legs. 'I think I'll go to bed.'

No sooner had Saskia left the room than the door opened again. Michael held onto the doorhandle and looked at the floor as he spoke.

'Thought I might have another go at that game.'

Jennifer and Andrew exchanged a glance. She carefully hid any hint of a smile. 'Sure, Mike. Light out in fifteen minutes, though.'

'OK.' Michael picked up the laptop and closed the living-room door behind him.

Andrew was grinning broadly when Jennifer caught his gaze again. 'I knew he wouldn't be able to hold out for long.'

'It's lovely to see him interested in something.' Jennifer smiled. 'Especially something that's just for himself. Something fun.'

'He's a serious kid,' Andrew agreed. 'But I can't say I'm surprised. He was old enough to be badly affected by his mother's death.'

'Actually, I think it was a worse blow when his dad left,' Jennifer said. She raised her eyebrows. 'How much have Saskia and the children told you about things?'

'Not that much,' Andrew responded. 'I know that the children's mother was your older sister. Janet, was it?'

Jennifer nodded.

'And that she was ill for a long time with cancer before she died and that their father...'

'Philip,' Jennifer supplied.

'That Philip couldn't handle the situation after Janet died and has gone to live in Australia.'

Jennifer shook her head slightly. 'That's not anywhere near the full story, though I can imagine it's what Sass has picked up locally. People have very short memories about some things.' Jennifer sighed sadly. 'Philip's a fantastic man,' she told Andrew. 'He came here to work about twelve years ago and single-handedly kept the family farm going after my father died. Mum got sick after he married Janet so they moved in here to look after her. It wasn't easy. Mum had very hard to control diabetes and she went completely blind, but she was independent and terribly stubborn right to the end. They managed by themselves until Janet had the twins and then it all became a bit much. That was when I decided to take a year and work out here as a GP.'

'You went to Christchurch hospital for your houseman years, didn't you?'

Jennifer nodded. 'So did Hamish. It wasn't a huge commuting time so we thought we'd still see each other at weekends. We were both so busy that I didn't think it would change things that much.'

'But it did?'

'I guess so.' Jennifer chewed her bottom lip thoughtfully. 'Hamish couldn't understand me putting my family ahead of him. He was prepared to cut me some slack but became more and more impatient. Then I discovered he was seeing someone else.' Jennifer smiled ruefully. 'Our relationship was habit more than anything. All those years of being engaged without ever getting around to getting married. It was remarkably easy to let go. Almost a relief.' Jennifer lapsed into a silence that Andrew finally broke.

'And you stayed here? What happened to those ambitions of working overseas? Becoming a surgeon?'

'It was nearly two years before Mum died and by then I'd discovered that I rather liked working here. My family history goes way back to the first settlers and it's always been home for me. On top of that, Janet became unwell. She discovered a lump in her breast and had to go through all the trauma of treatment for breast cancer after it was confirmed to be malignant. Janet needed me. Philip and the children needed me.'

Jennifer took the poker and pushed a log further into the fire. 'We thought she'd beaten the cancer. Angus was born the following year. The later stages of her pregnancy masked symptoms that were, in fact, the return of her cancer. Only this time it was worse. The spread included the liver.'

'That must have been rough. Especially with a new baby.'

'Angus never really knew Jan. I suspect he's always thought I was his mother. Even the twins turned to me more and more as Janet got sicker. It was a very slow process. She hung on for nearly two years. It was Michael who was the most affected. And Philip,' Jennifer added. 'He was suffering from depression even before Jan died but he still held things together—just. It was me that suggested he take some time out away from here and the children.' Jennifer's glance at Andrew was defensive. 'I didn't think he'd need this long to get things together and neither did he. He's stayed in close touch with the children and he hasn't abandoned them. He'll be back as soon as he's ready and they'll be a family again.'

Andrew was silent for a long time. Lost in her own memories, Jennifer continued to play with the fire. When Andrew spoke again, the soft words touched something very deep inside her.

'Are you happy, Jen?'

Jennifer was tempted to respond lightly. Positively. To say of course she was. She loved the children and Saskia had been a real bonus. But when was the last time someone had asked her that question and been genuinely interested in an honest answer? Even Hamish had never bothered making sure he knew the truth. As long as he'd been happy he'd assumed that she'd been as well.

'I love my work,' Jennifer finally answered. 'And I love my home. I have a lot of people that I care about very deeply and I'm never alone, so I can't be...' Her voice trailed off with a vague tone of surprise.

'Lonely?'

Jennifer shook her head. 'Silly thing to say. Especially to you.'

'Why?'

'We hardly know each other,' Jennifer said carefully. 'Not as friends, anyway. And here I am telling you something that I hadn't even realised myself. Something that sounds, oh, I don't know...ungrateful, I suppose. Here I have an interesting and challenging career, a beautiful home and wonderful children sharing my life. How could I possibly feel lonely?'

'Very easily,' Andrew said quietly. The very notion of Jennifer feeling lonely made him want to gather her in his arms. To hold her so close she would know that she never needed to feel lonely again. He knew exactly how she felt. And he knew the reason. 'You don't have a partner,' he added.

'I do. Brian Wallace. He came here to see you the first day you were sick. Don't you remember?'

'I'm not talking about a professional partner. I'm talking about a life partner. An equal relationship. Someone to love and be loved by. You nurture and care for a lot of people, Jen. Isn't there someone who can do that for you?'

'A man, you mean?' Jennifer grinned. 'As if!' She spread her hands. 'Look at me. I'm the old woman in the shoe. What man in their right mind would set foot in this place?'

'Me,' Andrew answered promptly. 'See? I'm here.'

Jennifer laughed. 'You were definitely not in your right mind when you arrived and you're still too weak to escape.'

'I'm not in any hurry to escape,' Andrew said quietly. 'I like it here.'

Jennifer's face stilled. She held Andrew's gaze for a heartbeat longer than was comfortable. A flush of colour crept into her cheeks as she looked away. 'We like having you here. And you're welcome to stay just as long as you want.'

Andrew let his gaze remain on Jennifer's profile as the glow from the fire played on her face and highlighted the golden glints in her hair. Her words had been polite. Friendly. But Jennifer seemed distracted. Almost embarrassed. Had he given away too much in that glance they'd shared?

Did Jennifer have any idea at all of the implications of her invitation? He could stay as long as he wanted.

Andrew Stephenson wanted for ever.

CHAPTER SIX

IT TOOK another two days for Andrew Stephenson to fulfil his end of the deal.

And by that time Jennifer's opinion of Andrew had changed to the point that her remembered prejudice was unrecognisable. How could she have ever considered this man to be arrogant? Sure, he assumed the mantle of leadership but the ease with which he did so came from the desire to achieve a successful outcome for everyone involved, not from any determination to prove himself superior. Jennifer had never seen him assume control outside a professional encounter until now, but the last few days had cast Andrew in the role of a hero in her unusual household.

It had been Andrew that had saddled up the fat little Welsh pony, Button, on the sunny Saturday afternoon so that the small tribe of children had been able to take turns being led along the still soggy pathways through the native bush bordering the creek on Jennifer's property. He had declared himself fit for the gentle exercise and that it was, in fact, the perfect prescription to rebuild his physical strength. Jennifer had been grateful for the offer, having been called in to see a patient she was becoming concerned about. Susan Begg had been suffering some distressing episodes of shortness of breath over the last few months and feeling generally tired and unwell. A near fainting spell had prompted the call to Jennifer on Saturday and she had arranged to meet Susan at the hospital to give her a thorough check-up.

Button was back in his paddock by the time Jennifer returned home. The pony was looking a lot better, having been brushed clear of the mud clogging his heavy winter coat. She had seen and waved at Saskia and the younger children, having passed them walking Sam home. Andrew and Michael were found sitting in the living room, huddled over the screen of the laptop.

'Beating the giant spiders again?'

'No.' Michael sounded scornful. 'Drew's showing me stas-stick—'

'Statistical analysis,' Andrew supplied helpfully. 'We're making graphs based on percentage analysis of data.'

'Really?' Jennifer was genuinely impressed. 'What sort of data?'

'Pollution,' Michael answered. 'It's my school project. I'm making a pie chart right now. I've got the bits for how much comes from cars and how much from coal fires and...' He took his eyes off the screen to glance at Andrew. 'How do I change the colour for this bit?'

'Highlight the area,' Andrew instructed. 'Then go to your toolbar. That's the strip up the top there. Click on colour and then choose.'

Michael used the mouse confidently. His face lit up with a grin as the section of the pie chart changed to green. 'This is cool,' he exclaimed. 'My project's going to be even better than Hannah's.'

'Who's Hannah?' Andrew queried.

'A girl in my class,' Michael said, his tone heavy with disgust. 'She thinks she's so smart.'

Andrew's glance met Jennifer's. Was Andrew empathising with having feminine competition in an academic arena? She caught a glint of real amusement and something more. An acknowledgement of their old relationship and perhaps a recognition that it had been less than mature? And Jennifer had once considered this man to be oblivious to the finer feelings of those around him. The glance was brief.

'And is she smart?' he asked Michael.

'I suppose.' Michael's agreement was grudging. He was clearly distracted. 'Hey, how are we going to print this out?'

'Save it to disk,' Jennifer suggested, as Andrew frowned in thought. 'I can take it to the hospital and print it out for you.' She eased the heavy bag from her shoulder and placed it on the end of the table. The ECG tracing she had taken from Susan Begg was in there, along with the cardiology textbooks she wanted to consult. 'Like a coffee?' she asked Andrew. 'I'm just going to make one for myself.'

'Thanks.' Andrew smiled. 'I could use one.'

He looked tired, which was hardly surprising, having spent his first full day out of bed. It wasn't just the children he'd been helping either. Jennifer was surprised to find an impressive array of peeled and shredded vegetables on the kitchen bench. A basin of finely sliced meat was marinading in what smelt like soy sauce. Jennifer sniffed appreciatively.

'We found an old wok.' Andrew's voice came from close behind her. 'I'm going to show Saskia how to do a stir-fry.' He reached to replace the basin's cover, his hand brushing Jennifer's. She hastily turned her attention back to the coffee, disconcerted by the level of her awareness the casual touch had invoked.

'How are you feeling?' she enquired briskly. 'You look a bit weary.'

'I am,' Andrew admitted. 'I'll probably fall asleep in the middle of my dinner. I've moved my stuff out into the cottage, by the way. You can have your own bed back.'

'Oh…thanks.' Jennifer felt suddenly embarrassed. Maybe it was just the thought that she would be sleeping in a bed recently vacated by Andrew. It would be impossible not to think of him as she lay there. Had he thought of her in the long hours he'd spent lying in her bed? The heat generated by her embarrassment was spreading. It lodged, inexplicably, low down in her abdomen. Jennifer searched for a way to change the subject.

'How's that cut on your leg doing?' She handed Andrew a mug of coffee. 'We'll be able to take those stitches out in a day or two.' Her cheeks still felt warm. This probably wasn't the ideal subject to tone down her awareness of Andrew's body. Thankfully, he seemed unaware of her discomfiture.

'It's nice and clean. Healing well. You did a great job.' Andrew sipped his coffee. 'How did you get on with that patient you went in to see?'

'Susan?' Jennifer was delighted to have an opportunity to both change the subject and discuss the case. It might even save her bothering

Brian at home for a second opinion. 'Come and see what you think of her ECG.'

Minutes later, one end of the table was spread with opened textbooks and patient record sheets. Michael was still in front of the laptop, looking very studious, at the other end of the table.

'So how long has she been having these spells?'

'A lot longer than I initially knew about. The first visits were just for persistent lethargy. She thought she was just run-down after having three children in as many years. It wasn't until she got really short of breath one day when she was hanging out the washing that I really started to take some notice, but I didn't pick up the murmur then.'

'So you're thinking maybe aortic stenosis?' Andrew picked up the ECG tracing again. 'It's a long time since I did much cardiology. Definitely a left bundle branch block. And these Q waves are quite marked.'

'What bothers me is that her father died suddenly when he was fifty-two. He was a top-dressing pilot and his plane crashed and then

burned so an autopsy was never done. What if
he crashed because he had some sort of cardiac
event? This trace and Susan's symptoms make
me wonder about something like hypertrophic
cardiomyopathy. If it is, then Susan's at risk
of sudden collapse and death at any time.
She's only twenty-six and she's got three kids
under five.'

'Are you going to refer her?'

Jennifer nodded. 'I'm keeping her in hospital for the weekend for a rest and then I'll
send her over to Christchurch to see a cardiologist on Monday. They can do further investigations, like an echo and catheterisation,
if necessary. I'm wondering if I should start
her on a beta blocker right now. Just to be on
the safe side. I was planning to read up on it
tonight.'

'I wouldn't mind reading up on it myself.'
Andrew sat down at the table and pulled a textbook towards himself. 'I'd forgotten how interesting all this is. You kind of lose the feel
of general medicine when you get caught up
in a specialty. Particularly surgery.' Andrew

grinned. 'The longest time you spend with your patients is when they're sound asleep.'

Jennifer was still staring at the ECG trace. It wasn't exactly a textbook example of abnormalities. They could have argued the significance of almost any part of it. Andrew could have quizzed her about her investigation of the murmur she'd heard. Whether she'd accurately determined if it was systolic or diastolic. If a fourth heart sound was clear and whether the abnormal heart sound diminished with the patient in a squatting position and increased markedly on standing. They could have argued the toss about the possibilities of mitral regurgitation or aortic stenosis. He could have dismissed her diagnosis on the basis of an imaginative interpretation of Susan's father's death or based on the need for more intensive investigation.

In the old days that was precisely the way they would have interacted. It was a revelation that Andrew could be as supportive as he could be challenging. Did the difference come because of the attitude with which Jennifer had approached the discussion or had she blown things out of all proportion in the past? And, if so, why?

Much to Jennifer's disappointment, the opportunity for any further discussion was lost as the noise level outside the house suddenly became impossible to ignore and the twins bounded into the living room.

'Hey, Drew! We found a *hedgehog*!'

'Did you?'

'It's only a baby. It might be sick. Can you come and have a look?'

Sophie was peering over Michael's shoulder. 'That spider just ate you,' she announced. 'Can I have a go?'

'When I'm finished,' Michael told her. 'This is a cool game.'

'Come *on*, Drew. Sass is finding a box for the hedgehog.' Jessica was pulling at Andrew's sleeve.

'I want to see it, too.' Michael finally wrenched himself away from the computer screen. The children all rushed from the room, with Andrew in tow. He managed a faintly apologetic grin in Jennifer's direction as he was borne away. She stared after them feeling slightly bewildered. The twins hadn't even said hello. She was a doctor. She could have managed a consultation on a potentially sick hedgehog with at least as much expertise as Andrew.

Jennifer's gaze caught the abandoned laptop. So much for the project and looking so studious. Michael was back to simply enjoying himself with the game. And he looked so happy. Was it Andrew's computer that was drawing Michael out of his shell with such stunning results or was it the relationship he was forming with this man? And what about all those vegetables in the kitchen? Why hadn't she taken the time to give Saskia cooking lessons instead of just stocking the pantry and freezer with plenty of fail-proof commercial products? Was Andrew trying to show up her failure as the head of this unusual family?

The twinge of resentment would have been easy to catch and enlarge. It was exactly how Jennifer would have interpreted Andrew's behaviour in years gone by but she knew now, with absolute certainty, that she would be wrong in doing so. Andrew wasn't trying to prove anything. He was being drawn into the family because of who he was. Jennifer smiled to herself rather wryly. She might as well go with the flow and enjoy it along with all the others. It wasn't as though it was going to last very long.

The tiny hedgehog shouldn't have been out of the nest at all. It was the size of a golf ball under its still soft prickles. The eyes were firmly closed and the tiny black feet and legs lacked the strength to keep the baby animal upright for more than a few seconds at a time. Named Sonic by Michael, their new pet was fed from an eyedropper with some of the black kitten's special cat milk and a nest was made in a shoebox with hay and one of Michael's rugby socks. The excitement over the new family member overrode the children's appreciation of the dinner but Jennifer was well aware of how proud Saskia felt.

'This is fantastic,' she congratulated the teenager.

'It was fun. I never knew how easy it was to cook.'

Andrew's exhaustion didn't prevent him offering to keep Sonic's shoebox beside his bed and setting his alarm clock to ensure that he woke often enough to keep up the two-hourly feeding schedule he'd proposed.

Jennifer made a quick trip to the hospital on Sunday morning, primarily to check on Susan, and returned to find that Andrew had been persuaded to attend Michael's rugby game that afternoon. They were to be collected by Tom Bartlett, whose son Lawrence was also in Michael's team.

'You don't need to come if you don't want to,' Michael told Jennifer. The boy didn't meet his aunt's eye and the casual tone was careful enough to make Jennifer pause. She always went to watch the games if possible. It gave her a chance to spend time with Michael and he'd needed the push to keep up his interest in the game after his father had no longer been on the sideline to cheer for his son's team. Today, Michael was already dressed in his kit an hour before he needed to be. The fact that his studded rugby boots were clean was nothing short of a miracle. Was the enthusiasm due to the fact that he had a male figure coming to watch who might be able to appreciate the finer points of the game? Or was it that Andrew wouldn't stand out as being different from the gathering of local fathers and boys that normally edged the field?

'I might give it a miss just for once.' Jennifer tried to match Michael's casual tone. 'I could do with catching up on a bit of house-work.'

Michael just nodded. 'We might be a bit late back,' he added. 'Lawrence's dad said he might take Drew to the pub for a beer after the game. Lawrence and I can go and play on the beach.'

It was dusk by the time they returned. Jennifer was sweeping the verandah. She paused and leaned on the broom as Andrew mounted the steps.

'How was the game?'

'A resounding success. I forget the score but Mike's team won by a mile.'

'Thirty-two to twelve,' Michael shouted tri-umphantly. He clattered across the wooden verandah, dropping mud from his boots as he headed towards the front door.

'That's great,' Jennifer told him. 'But take those boots *off* before you go inside.'

It took another minute to sweep up the debris Michael had left. Andrew wandered to the clean end of the verandah to stay out of Jennifer's way. He leaned on the railing, gazing down from the vantage point the house provided, seeming content to admire the view of the sunset over the harbour and hills. Jennifer propped the broom beside the door.

'Beautiful, isn't it?'

Andrew nodded. 'This is an amazing little corner of the world. I've never been here before despite the time I've spent in Christchurch. I always thought I had to leave the country to find the best parts of the world.'

Jennifer smiled. 'What is it they say? Don't leave town till you've seen the country. We often ignore the things right under our noses. They become ordinary because of the familiarity.' She joined Andrew at the railing. 'How did you get on with Tom?'

'He's a nice guy. I enjoyed our session at the pub. He introduced me to a few locals.' Andrew glanced sideways with a grin. 'You were a popular subject for conversation. I heard a lot about you.'

'All good, I hope,' Jennifer said lightly.

Andrew's gaze was now thoughtful. 'They think the world of you around here. And they're proud of you. I almost got the impression of ownership.'

Jennifer shrugged modestly. 'I'm one of them. My family has always been here. As a doctor I get involved in people's lives. Sometimes it's not a good thing. It can become too personal which makes it difficult to be objective.'

'Talking about personal, I met one chap who reckons he should be your grandfather by rights.'

Jennifer laughed. 'That would have to be Charlie.'

'I can't remember his name. I got introduced to too many people.'

'Looks like a gnome? Very short with a rim of fluffy white hair and he's ancient. Could pass for about a hundred and ten, though he's only in his nineties.'

'That's him. He was wearing an oilskin coat and gumboots. Looked rather strange.'

'He was a fisherman. Still hangs out around the boats. He's as tough as they come. I wouldn't be surprised if he does live well past a hundred. He can trace his stock back to the whalers that came from Normandy. He reckons his mother was born on the *Comte de Paris* which was the ship that brought the first settlers to Akaroa in 1840. There's no record of the birth, though, and she would have been a bit old by the time he was born, but nobody wants to point that out to Charlie.'

'So what's with the grandfather bit?'

'That could be his imaginative version of history as well. He says he was engaged to my grandmother until my grandfather stole her away.'

'Not true?'

'I have my doubts. One thing I do remember about Gran is that she couldn't stand the smell of fish. I suspect the prospect of being the wife of a fisherman wouldn't have held much appeal.'

'What did your grandfather do?'

'Took over the farm from his father who *was* one of the first settlers. He cleared this land himself, married an English girl a few years later and they had twelve children. I've got people who are related to me in some way all over the countryside.'

'So you've got a good dose of French blood? Do you feel any connection with that part of your heritage?'

'Hard not to around here. The French connection is something that Akaroa is proud of. The street names, the architecture, even some of the original trees are being carefully preserved.'

'I think it was Charlie who claimed that everyone should actually be speaking French in these parts. Your ancestors were all cheated.'

Jennifer laughed. 'It's true in a way. A Frenchman came here on a whaling ship in 1838 and decided that the peninsula would be the perfect place to start the French colonisation of the South Island. He apparently made a deed of purchase with local Maori chiefs, went back home and got backing from the French government, which led to the arrival of the first ship carrying settlers. They arrived to find that the Treaty of Waitangi had been signed only a couple of days earlier and that they were now in a British colony. My great-grandfather was one of those settlers. He did hang onto his native language enough to make sure his children were fluent. I remember my grandfather could curse wonderfully in French.'

'Must be quite special to have so much of a bond with a place. Somewhere that has such deep ties to your own family history.' Andrew took another long glance at the panoramic view as the light faded even further. He sighed almost imperceptibly. 'I haven't got anything like that. My mother remarried when I was seven. We'd been on the move for years before that and I have no memories at all of my father. I certainly never felt like I belonged after that. I was an outsider but nobody bothered telling me where I *did* belong.'

'Must have been tough.' Jennifer could hear the children in the house behind them and was reminded that it was well past time to prepare dinner. Saskia would be busy bathing her baby. Jennifer was also reminded of the rapport the teenager and Andrew had achieved in such a short time. And no wonder. 'I can see why Saskia finds you such a sympathetic ear,' she told Andrew. 'It's good that she has someone to talk to who can really understand.'

'She's going to be OK. Did she tell you that her father is coming to visit her tomorrow? I'm going to look after Angus and Vanessa when she goes to meet him for lunch in town. She wasn't sure she wanted him to see where she was living—just in case things don't work out.'

'I hope they do,' Jennifer said fervently.

'Maybe she'll want to go back home. How would you manage without her?'

'Goodness knows,' Jennifer said. 'I guess we'll just have to face that crisis if and when it arrives. I'm sure we'd manage. Fielding crises is all part of the plot around here.'

*   *   *

Minor crises did indeed crop up with customary frequency that evening. Angus tripped over Zippy and gave himself a painful bump on his forehead. The twins squabbled furiously over whose turn it was to feed Sonic, and Vanessa decided she wasn't going to go to sleep. The baby was screaming vigorously long after the twins and Angus had gone to bed. Michael was sulking because Andrew had banned him from playing on the computer. Jennifer met them on the stairs as she took a dose of paracetamol up to Vanessa. The new tooth coming through was clearly painful enough to be causing tonight's disturbance and Saskia was tired and wanted to go to bed herself.

'Time for bed, Mike,' Jennifer said in passing. 'Don't forget to clean your teeth.'

'Oh, but—'

'No buts,' Jennifer added firmly. She could hear Vanessa's crying gaining magnitude. 'Get a move on.'

Michael scowled but Jennifer was surprised that his look was directed at Andrew. Andrew seemed unperturbed.

'We made a deal, remember?' he said calmly. 'You were going to clean your rugby boots and *then* you could have a game on the computer before bedtime.'

'I could clean them now,' Michael offered quickly.

'Too late, I'm afraid. Jen says it's bedtime.'

Jennifer was tempted to offer another ten minutes but she stopped herself, curious to see how Michael would deal with the gentle discipline. Andrew was waiting for Michael to catch him up at the foot of the stairs.

'A deal's a deal, Mike. You have to keep your end of the bargain, and that includes keeping to time. It's very important to be a man of your word.'

Michael was in bed five minutes later. Jennifer grinned at Andrew when she went back downstairs to find him sitting by the fire. 'You're a hard man, Andrew Stephenson.'

'Is he upset?'

'He's looked resigned rather than aggrieved.' Jennifer curled herself up on the hearthrug and reached out to stroke the dogs with a contented sigh. 'This is good,' she re-marked. 'My favourite part of the day.'

'I hope you don't think I'm interfering,' Andrew told her. 'With Michael, I mean.'

'Not at all,' Jennifer assured him. 'You're doing wonders for Mike.' She cast Andrew a speculative glance. 'It's just a shame you don't practise what you preach.'

'What?' Andrew looked startled.

'A deal's a deal, is it?' Jennifer bit back her smile.

'Of course.'

'So when are you going to get around to keeping the deal you made with me? I kept my end of the bargain. I told you my story about why I never married Hamish. You, however, have not enlightened me about what I wanted to know.'

'Which was?' Andrew looked uncomfort-able. 'I was pretty sick, you know. I could have been delirious at the time.'

Jennifer wasn't going to let him escape. Her curiosity had surfaced again in this time of do-mestic peace and she was determined to learn more about Andrew. The desire to know more—preferably on a personal level—was surprising in its intensity. 'You agreed to tell me why you gave up practising medicine,' she said quietly. 'And why you were on honeymoon with a non-existent wife. A deal's a deal, Andrew,' she added solemnly. 'So tell!'

Andrew was silent for a long moment. Jennifer waited, rubbing Elvis's silky ear as the dog settled against her. She began to wonder whether she should have pushed quite so soon. Maybe the story was too painful to tell. She didn't want to cause this man any pain. In fact, she was aware of a ridiculous urge to protect Andrew—to tell him that it really didn't matter and if he didn't want to talk about it, that was fine. On the point of opening her mouth, Jennifer's reassurance was pre-empted by Andrew's sigh of resignation.

'It's the same story, in a way. I'm just not sure where to begin.'

'Start with the last time I heard any news about you,' Jennifer encouraged, her reluctance evaporating. 'It must have been about three years ago when you left the Boston Memorial and went private.'

'Seems like as good a place as any. That's certainly where it all began.' Andrew shook his head. 'I should have stayed at the Memorial. I might have been overworked and relatively underpaid but I was happy enough.'

'Why did you leave, then?'

'The lure of fame and fortune, I guess. The head surgeon at the J.J. Shuster Institute of Health was a man called William Chadwick. William James Chadwick the third, no less. Extremely wealthy, highly sought after, connected with local politics. The works. I was flattered to be chosen by him to join the team. They had a well-deserved reputation for brilliance and it was just the sort of unit I'd always dreamed of belonging to back in medical school days.'

'You and me both.' Jennifer smiled. 'So it wasn't all it was cracked up to be?'

'Oh, initially it was. It was fantastic. Interesting cases, superb facilities. A great team to work with. Very friendly, very dedicated and all very loyal to William Chadwick. I was one of them. I made an incredible amount of money doing what I loved doing.

My social life took a leap into an echelon I'd never expected, and I became engaged to Chadwick's daughter, Cassandra. She'd been a cheerleader at college and then a model for a while. By the time we were introduced she was over thirty and probably under pressure to settle down and produce William James Chadwick the fourth. Her father pushed us both into the relationship but neither of us really resisted. He was like that. He got his own way but he did it with such charm and successful results that everyone eventually fell into line.'

'Did you love Cassandra?'

Andrew gave Jennifer a slow glance. 'Not in the way you should if you're going to share someone's life, but I didn't have anyone like that and I didn't think I ever would. It might have been less than perfect but it was better than nothing. In fact, it was better than anything I'd ever had. I actually felt like I belonged somewhere for the first time in my life. These people wanted *me*—or so I thought. I went along with the plans for a huge wedding. We were allotted a twelve-month engagement to allow time for the preparations. Cassie thought the idea of a honeymoon travelling around New Zealand in a camper van was cute so I made the bookings more than a year ago.' Andrew sighed heavily. 'I must have been blind. Maybe it was lucky I found out before it was too late.'

'Found out what, precisely?'

'That I was being used. That I was highly expendable and they really didn't give a damn about me.'

'How did you find out?'

'There was a huge social occasion that Cassie and I attended, along with William Chadwick. A senator who was his closest friend was celebrating some political triumph. The evening turned into a disaster when the senator's fairly recent and much younger wife suddenly collapsed. The senator, William and I rushed her off to the hospital where it became evident that she had a haemorrhage from a duodenal ulcer and required urgent surgery. The senator insisted that nobody but William was going to operate on his wife. I tried to stop him. We'd both been drinking that evening but

William was in charge as usual and swept ahead with the arrangements. He wanted me to assist. I wasn't happy but I'd had much less than him to drink and William made it clear that my future was on the line.'

'That's appalling,' Jennifer breathed. 'He threatened to fire you?'

'He was angry. I'd suggested he wasn't fit to operate and nobody ever criticised William. I'd made the mistake of suggesting we call in another member of the team in front of an influential friend. The senator was as amazed as William that I could have the nerve to think someone else could do a better job.'

'I take it the surgery didn't go well?'

'The woman died,' Andrew said flatly. 'William not only bungled the surgery but when she started bleeding out he panicked. He wouldn't let me, or anyone else, get near the woman and he failed totally to control the situation. By the time I actually knocked him out of the way, it was too late.'

Jennifer was staring, wide-eyed. 'And you took the blame?'

'You said it. William's story was that he realised he'd had too much alcohol to be safe and that I claimed not to have had anything at all to drink. And that I did the surgery myself.'

'But there were other people there! Theatre staff—the anaesthetist, nurses. Witnesses.'

'William's people. They fell into line. He managed everything ruthlessly. He even had the police take a blood sample from me so that they could proved I had been lying about my alcohol intake. The results were hardly damning but they *were* positive. And that's not something I'm proud of.'

'So you got fired.' Jennifer's words fell into the heavy silence.

'I got sued. I lost everything I owned and more. My reputation was ruined. I'm still waiting for the official result of the malpractice suit and being possibly struck off the medical register. I lost my career and my future. And, of course, Cassandra dumped me very quickly and very publicly. The newspapers and television had the sort of feast the Americans enjoy so much. There were famous names involved and such a clear scapegoat.'

Jennifer shook her head with disbelief. 'And nobody spoke up for you?'

'Nobody.'

Andrew didn't meet Jennifer's eyes. Her reaction to his story was profound. She believed his version of the events completely and the thought that he'd received no support—from anybody—wrenched something deep inside her. She reached out and took Andrew's hand. Maybe she wanted to let him know that not everybody could be so callous. Maybe she wanted to let him know she understood—and cared. Andrew's hand gripped hers and for nearly a minute they simply sat there holding hands. They sat in complete silence but Jennifer knew that her message had been received and understood. The brief glance that Andrew gave her when he released her hand was one of gratitude.

'I think I'd better head off to bed.' Andrew's smile was wry. 'I had no idea that being a man of one's word could be so exhausting.'

'Sleep well,' Jennifer said gently. 'And, Andrew?'

'Mmm?'

'Thanks for telling me. It can't have been an easy thing to talk about.'

Andrew held her gaze and then shook his head slowly. 'I left the States as soon as I could and just kept moving. I haven't spoken to anyone about it since then. And even when it was all hitting the fan I never had anyone to tell. No one whose opinion mattered.'

Jennifer's smile was shy. She liked the idea that her opinion mattered. Andrew turned to leave but stopped at Jennifer's soft call.

'Drew?'

'Mmm?'

'I'm glad you told me.'

Andrew looked solemn. 'A deal's a deal.'

Jennifer was smiling now. 'And you're a man of your word.'

'Absolutely.' The gaze they held went on. And on. Jennifer didn't know which of them broke the eye contact but it really didn't matter. The message was there and clearly received on both sides.

'Sleep well, Jen.'

Jennifer made no response other than a smile. She doubted whether she would sleep at all well. The web of circumstances that had pulled her closer to Andrew Stephenson had just become a great deal tighter. She was being drawn close enough to want the contact on a much more personal level. She wanted to touch and be touched. The heightened awareness Jennifer had noticed around Andrew had just exploded into a physical desire the likes of which Jennifer had never contemplated the possibility of experiencing.

Jennifer closed her eyes. Her sigh came out as a faint groan. Sleep well, indeed. Fat chance of that!

CHAPTER SEVEN

IT WAS only a matter of time now.

Time and opportunity. The sexual energy that charged the atmosphere was so noticeable to Jennifer that she was amazed it didn't stop everybody else in their tracks. Like nurse Wendy Granger who ushered Andrew into the treatment room early on Monday afternoon. Or Dr Brian Wallace, who poked his head through the doorway a few minutes later just as Jennifer had removed the dressing on Andrew's leg.

'You're looking a hell of a lot better than the last time I saw you,' he told Andrew.

'I feel great.' Andrew smiled.

Jennifer, who had her hands on his leg, feeling for inflammation around the edges of the wound, silently agreed. And she knew precisely what it was that was making Andrew's skin feel so alive under her fingertips. She had an interest in this particular patient that was far from professional.

'Jennifer was pretty worried about you for a few days there.' Brian had moved closer to peer at the wound on Andrew's leg. 'That was a rather decent cut you had. Nice job of stitching, Jen.'

'Thanks. They're ready to come out now. It shouldn't leave too much of a scar.'

Brian was looking rather wistful. 'Wish I'd been here. I do enjoy a spot of stitching.'

'You should have been a surgeon,' Andrew suggested.

'I was—to some extent,' Brian told him. 'Back in the old days when I first started practising here we were a real cottage hospital. We had a theatre. My partner had anaesthetics training and we did quite a lot of minor stuff. Hernias and tonsils, for example.' He watched Jennifer catch the ends of a stitch with tweezers and slide a scalpel through the loop to sever the thread. She pulled the stitch clear and dropped it into a kidney dish. 'I did a Caesarean once,' Brian continued. 'But I never tried a splenectomy. Wish I'd been here,' he repeated.

'It's just as well you had the history of surgery here,' Andrew said, 'otherwise we wouldn't have had the equipment we needed for Liam.'

'I've kept it in good shape.' Brian nodded proudly. 'More for the sake of nostalgia than anything, but it certainly paid off for Liam Bellamy.'

Jennifer had the fourth stitch in her tweezers now. It was caught in well-healed skin and Andrew winced slightly as she pulled the knot clear. 'Sorry. Won't be much longer.'

'I'll leave you to it,' Brian excused himself. 'Come and have a coffee when you're through, Andrew, and I'll show you the old surgery records. If you're interested, that is.'

'Sure. I'd like that.'

Jennifer could feel the atmosphere change as Brian left the room. She concentrated on her task. Only a couple more stitches to come out and she could clean the odd spot of dried blood from the wound and perhaps dress it with—

'Are you listening to me, Jen?'

'Of course.' Jennifer glanced up, colour flooding her cheeks as she realised that the enjoyable tones of Andrew's voice had been flowing over her without her catching more than a word or two. 'You're talking about Sass.'

'And her dad.' Andrew was watching Jennifer carefully. 'And the fact that she wants to go back to Christchurch with him for a few days.'

'Oh.' Jennifer digested the information as she reached for a gauze swab and a bottle of antiseptic. 'I'm so glad the meeting went well.'

'Sass brought him back to the house to meet his granddaughter. It was love at first sight for both of them. She's packing a bag right now.'

'She's leaving today?' Jennifer's jaw dropped. 'That doesn't give me much time to find anyone to help with the children.' Distracted, Jennifer swabbed at Andrew's leg, a worried frown crinkling her forehead. 'Where's Angus and what about meeting the other children after school? I've got a clinic. I can't just cancel it and I don't want Brian having to take over. I can't believe Sass would take off just like this.'

'Calm down,' Andrew told her. 'Saskia wasn't just going to leave you in the lurch. I told her it was OK.'

'What?' Jennifer's head jerked up. 'Why did you say that? It's not OK. I need time to organise my life if Saskia's leaving.' Jennifer's anxiety turned to anger. 'You've got no right to—'

'Hold it!' Andrew held up a hand to emphasise the command. He sat up, swinging his legs over the side of the bed so he was now looking down at Jennifer. He held her gaze and spoke firmly. 'Saskia is not leaving for ever. This will be a short visit. She wasn't even going to consider leaving the children until I told her that I was quite happy to step into her shoes. I can do everything she normally does. However...' Andrew paused, his voice still stern. 'I draw the line at purple dreadlocks and a nose ring.'

Jennifer laughed. Her anger dissipated. The anxiety diminished but didn't fade entirely.

'Are you sure you want to do that? It's a lot of work, caring for four children.'

'I seem to remember you told me I could stay as long as I wanted to. I want to help Sass out here. I know what it's like to lose your family for ever. She has the chance of repairing something important. If you'd seen the look on her face when her dad was cuddling Vanessa, you would have said exactly what I did. You would have told her to go home and spend time with her father.'

'You're right.' Jennifer took a deep breath. Then she smiled. 'You know something, Andrew Stephenson?'

'What's that?'

'You're a nice man. I never knew that about you.'

'You were always too busy arguing with me.'

'You always started it.' Expecting a contradiction, Jennifer was disarmed by Andrew's ready grin.

'It was the only way I could get your attention.'

He had her attention now. Every ounce of it. His face seemed to have moved a lot closer.

'Have you any idea,' Andrew queried softly, 'of just how jealous I was of Hamish Ryder?'

If Wendy hadn't been aware of the electrical atmosphere earlier, she couldn't avoid being confronted by it head on when she opened the door of the treatment room in the seconds following Andrew's words. They weren't actually kissing but there was no doubt at all in Wendy's mind that another split second would have closed that tiny gap between them. She flushed scarlet. 'Sorry…I should have knocked.'

Jennifer jumped visibly, stepping back from the bed and turning away from Andrew. She looked almost as embarrassed as her nurse. 'Is the ambulance here already?'

'No.' Wendy's glance strayed back towards Andrew. He grinned and Wendy smiled back. 'It's on its way. Susan's husband just popped home to get the hairbrush he'd forgotten. Susan's a bit worried about the ambulance trip, though, which is why I came to find you. She gets car-sick on the hill unless she's driving. She wants to know if she can take something.'

'Of course.' Jennifer moved to a wall cupboard and unlocked it. She selected an ampoule and syringe. 'This should last long enough for the trip. Give it intramuscularly now and it should be at maximum efficacy by the time they reach the hill.'

'Nice to see you again, Mr Stephenson,' Wendy said. Her glance was decidedly mischievous. 'Sorry I interrupted.'

'Call me Drew,' Andrew invited. 'And you didn't interrupt anything that won't keep.'

The kidney dish Jennifer was holding rattled disconcertingly. The time was here already. Only the opportunity was needed now.

The rest of the afternoon clinic went smoothly. Mrs Scallion's blood pressure was down and she wasn't experiencing any side effects from the medication. Her fasting glucose results had been abnormal and Jennifer started her on oral medication for diabetes as well as delivering her usual encouragement for her patient's weight loss programme. John Bellamy came in to have the stitches out of his hand and Jennifer was delighted to catch up on news of Liam.

'It's a relief to have him out of Intensive Care,' John told her. 'All those tubes and machines are too much for me.' He shook his head. 'He's complaining that it still hurts to breathe but I tell him he's bloody lucky to be breathing at all.'

'It'll take a while for all those broken ribs to come right. I'm not surprised Liam's finding it painful to breathe. He won't be going out on the boat with you anytime soon.'

John grinned. 'I don't think he's in too much of a hurry to even get home. He's got rather friendly with the nurses at that hospital.'

'I'll bet. He's a good-looking lad.'

'There's a male nurse in the orthopaedic ward he's moved to. Liam's got this idea that it might not be a bad sort of job. It's not that I want him to follow in my footsteps but...' John's face was a picture of mistrust. 'Seems like a pansyish sort of job for a bloke.'

'Don't you believe it,' Jennifer told him firmly. 'Nursing is a wonderful career and you can get a job anywhere in the world. Liam's a caring person. I've watched the way he's helped you with the younger children since Peggy died. He'd be great. And who knows? He might want a job here, and we're always on the lookout for good nurses.'

'Work here? You'd employ a man as a nurse?'

'Wouldn't hesitate for a moment. He might like to consider medical school as well. He could become a doctor.' Jennifer grinned. 'I'll need a new partner one of these days.'

'No way we could run to affording that kind of education.' John didn't flinch as the final stitch was pulled free. 'But maybe nursing's not such a bad idea.'

The clinic was over by four p.m. but Jennifer found some extra people in the waiting room. Saskia was sitting beside an older man who had Vanessa sitting on his lap.

'This is my dad, Jen. Drew said he told you about everything.'

'I'm delighted to meet you.' Jennifer's gaze was watchful. 'Ken, isn't it?'

The man nodded as he extended his hand. Jennifer took the firm grip. Vanessa gurgled and Ken took a moment to smile down at the baby. 'I can't thank you enough for what you've done for Sass. I'd never have left her alone if I'd known about the baby, you know.'

'And we wouldn't have had the pleasure of her company for the last year.' Jennifer smiled. 'We're going to miss Saskia.'

'It's only for a few days,' Saskia assured Jennifer. The teenager's face was radiating pride as she looked at her baby and her father. Pride and happiness. Jennifer doubted whether Saskia would ever come back for more than a visit and she hoped that it would work out that way. Andrew was right. The family bond was too important to lose—especially at Saskia's tender age.

'Anyway, Drew's cooking is heaps better than mine. He's doing roast chicken for you tonight.'

'Maybe you should stay for dinner,' Jennifer suggested.

'Kind of you, but we'd better head off.' Ken stood up, still holding Vanessa. 'We want to get back home before dark if we can.'

'Have you got everything you need for Vanessa? Did you take the car seat? What about nappies?'

'You've done so much already,' Saskia's father said. 'We'll borrow the car seat and buy anything else we need once we get back to town.'

Jennifer left the hospital a short time later. It felt odd driving home, knowing that Saskia wouldn't be there with the children. It felt even more odd when she drove into the yard and parked her vehicle beside the barn. The dogs were nowhere to be seen. Neither were any cats or children. On the verge of becoming anxious, Jennifer scanned the yard and its surroundings. All was quiet. Too quiet. The ducks on the paddock pond looked untroubled but the group of nearby birds were far less happy. A flock of disgruntled hens had been herded into the corner of Button's paddock and were now being guarded meticulously by Zippy. And if Zippy was there, Michael couldn't be far away. Her dogs chose the objects of their loyalty and once they'd chosen they were admirably faithful.

Rounding the corner of the barn, Jennifer found them all. The twins sat on either end of the water trough and Angus knelt between them, busy floating a plastic duck in the water. Elvis lay morosely to one side, his gaze skyward. Jennifer grinned as she followed the dog's line of vision. Andrew was perched on the roof of the henhouse facing Michael, who had nails held between his lips and a hammer in his hand.

'Mike's fixing the roof,' Sophie told Jennifer. 'Molly's nest won't get wet any more.'

'That's great. How was school, Jess?' Jennifer held out her arms to Angus who came running for a hug.

'Saskia's gone,' Jessica informed her. 'Who's going to read our story tonight?'

'I will,' Jennifer promised.

'Hi, Jen.' Andrew was concentrating on helping Michael. 'Hold the nail and tap it gently until it catches,' he advised. 'Then it's less likely to bend when you really hit it.'

Michael hadn't even noticed Jennifer's arrival. He took the last nail from his mouth. 'Do you reckon we'll need another shingle here, Drew?'

'I reckon.' Andrew handed one to the boy before looking down again. 'We'll be through here in a few minutes, Jen. Could you go and check the oven? I think the potatoes might need turning over.'

'Sure.' Jennifer took Angus's hand. 'Come and have your bath, Angus. Don't forget to bring yellow duckie.'

'We'll come, too,' Sophie declared. 'This is boring. Drew won't let us climb up on the roof.'

'I'm pleased to hear that.' Jennifer grinned. 'Did you collect the eggs?'

'No. We were too busy watching.'

'How 'bout you get the eggs and then come inside and wash your hands? It'll be teatime soon.'

The evening sped past. It seemed to take no time at all to feed and bathe the children, to supervise homework and read stories and get them all into bed. Michael offered to let Angus sleep in his room so he wouldn't feel lonely with Saskia and Vanessa gone. It took no time and yet it took for ever. Because as soon as the household had settled, Jennifer and Andrew were going to be alone. The time was here and with no one but peacefully sleeping children in the house—so was the opportunity.

And yet they waited. They washed the dishes and discussed the children and what needed to be done around the house the next day. After today's success with mending the henhouse roof, Andrew and Michael were now planning to build a treehouse and Andrew wanted to know where to go for hardware supplies. They talked about the patients Jennifer had seen at the hospital and what the investigations now scheduled for Susan Begg by the cardiology department might reveal. They sat by the fire later and shared the hope that Saskia and her father were starting to repair the damage of the last few years. Until, finally, they ran out of things to talk about and just sat in silence. A long, long silence that Andrew was the one to break.

'I'm in love with you, Jen,' he said softly. 'I always have been.'

The words seemed to hang in the air, radiating an energy that had the potential to transform Jennifer's life, if she dared to let it. Right now, she was having enough trouble catching a breath.

'I always thought you hated me.' Jennifer couldn't meet the gaze she knew was upon her. She could feel the echo of Andrew's words like a physical touch but she couldn't trust them. Not yet. There were too many memories of the antagonism that had always been between them. 'You never tried to be anything other than competitive.' Jennifer risked a quick glance towards Andrew. 'Ever. No matter what I did, you were trying to do better.'

'Maybe it was the only way I could attract your attention,' Andrew suggested with a gentle smile. 'I wouldn't have stood a chance with Hamish Ryder so keen. He was the golden boy. For you and everyone else.'

Jennifer had to admit the ploy had worked. She had never failed to notice Andrew Stephenson. Neither had she failed to notice the attention he had attracted from other women.

'You always had a girlfriend.' Her glance towards Andrew was challenging this time. 'Lots of them.'

'Maybe that was competition as well. You had Hamish. I didn't want you to think that nobody wanted me. And there were lots of them because there was never anyone special enough. Nobody that I wanted as much as I wanted you.' Andrew's tone dropped to a whisper. *'Nobody.'*

Jennifer caught these words. She absorbed them and allowed the intensity of her reaction a foothold.

'I wish I'd known.' Jennifer hesitated, momentarily overwhelmed by the significance of what she wanted to say. 'Maybe I felt the same way and just convinced myself I didn't because you were so obviously uninterested.' Her smile was almost shy. 'I certainly thought about you enough. Competing with you was the driving force that kept me going. I missed it after we graduated.'

Andrew stood up slowly. He stepped over Zippy and skirted Elvis so that he was standing in front of Jennifer. His gaze was very serious, his words utterly sincere.

'I love you.'

'I...love you, too.' Jennifer cleared her throat. It was time to trust. Time to risk exposing the same vulnerability that Andrew was trusting her with. 'I think I always did,' she told him softly. 'But I've only just realised it.'

Andrew held out his hands and drew Jennifer to her feet. She needed the support of his hands. Her legs felt dangerously unsupportive.

'I want you.' It was Andrew's turn to clear his throat. 'So much that it hurts.'

Jennifer was standing very close. She only had to lean forward a little further to be aware of how truthful Andrew was being. As the length of his body contacted hers she had to catch her breath at the overwhelming wave of her own desire. She couldn't have voiced her need—words had entirely deserted her—but the communication was clear enough in her face and body. The pressure of Andrew's body against hers increased and his hands held her face when his mouth claimed hers. The kiss was merely a hint of what either of them could expect, and they both knew it could only get better. Andrew pulled back, his gaze locked on Jennifer's.

'Let's go upstairs,' he suggested. 'I think it's time we went to bed.'

Their first night together was a seal on a declaration of love more profound than any other two people could have possibly experienced. The next two weeks confirmed that no other two people could have melded their lives so seamlessly. They belonged together. The connection had always been there—just waiting to be slotted together and locked into place. How else could Jennifer find an explanation for the fact that amidst the circus of children, animals and juggling a demanding full-time job, she suddenly had a refuge that provided laughter, safety and a physical fulfilment that only became more intense the more they learned about each other.

Each day seemed to hold a surprise that drew them closer together, weaving a bond of trust and love that appeared unshakable. Like Andrew's reaction on the day Jennifer was delayed by an emergency at the hospital. He voiced no resentment at having to cope alone for the evening. By the time Jennifer finally arrived home, the children were sound asleep. The living room was softly lit by a dozen fat candles. A hot supper was waiting by the fireside and Andrew's arms were waiting to welcome and reassure her.

A tension that had been part of her life for a long time evaporated as Jennifer was able to share the huge responsibility she had taken on with her sister's children. Although capable, Saskia had been little more than a child herself and Jennifer hadn't realised how much her background concern about her family had pervaded her professional life. Now she could relax, her confidence and trust in Andrew absolute, the unexpected spin-off being an even greater involvement and satisfaction in her work. Jennifer felt there was nothing that could possibly add to her happiness yet she fostered the secret knowledge that something probably would.

She wasn't wrong. Only a day or two later Andrew left Michael in charge of the younger children, saying that there was something important that Jennifer needed to be shown. The children were impressed by Andrew's solemn tone and promised to behave, but Jennifer was worried. What could have happened that Andrew didn't want the children to see? Had the pony, Button, injured himself on that loose bit of fencing near the pond? Had the hens been struck by an incurable illness?

Andrew was giving no clues, merely shaking his head at each of Jennifer's anxious queries. He led her by the hand, taking her down a track into the bush on the far side of the stream. Jennifer lapsed into silence. Maybe the high winter flow of the stream had caused subsidence that was threatening some of her favourite old trees. Preoccupied by her thoughts, Jennifer was momentarily puzzled when they stopped.

'What is it? What do I need to see?'

'Look around you,' Andrew suggested softly.

Jennifer looked. It took only seconds to understand why Andrew had brought her here. They were standing in the clearing that her grandmother had chosen as the place to plant bluebells. Over the years, the bulbs had multiplied to form a thick carpet, the blooming of which was an eagerly anticipated annual event. How could Jennifer have forgotten to monitor their progress this year? Had Andrew discovered the surprise today or had he been waiting to present the sight in its full glory? The gift was memorable. As memorable as the taste of his kiss, flavoured by the scent of a million tiny blue flowers.

The joy that Andrew and Jennifer were experiencing seemed to be contagious. Michael won a prize at school for his project on pollution and the family celebration clearly added to his new sense of pride in himself. Andrew supervised the twins as they baked a congratulatory chocolate cake. The children unanimously declared the cake to be delicious. The look exchanged by Andrew and Jennifer acknowledged the truth and hid the laughter they knew would be shared when the event was recalled in times to come. Only the adults knew that the theft of the leftover cake by Elvis and Zippy went unpunished.

The call from Saskia to deliver the not entirely unexpected decision to stay with her father was almost welcome. With no other adults in the house, the nights belonged entirely to Jennifer and Andrew. The call from the children's father, Philip, the following weekend made Jennifer smile.

'I think he might be jealous of you,' she told Andrew. 'He complained that this ''Drew'' was all the kids could tell him about. He said they weren't even excited about the visit he's planning for next month. He wanted to know who you were and what was so special about you.'

'What did you say?'

'I said that the children had helped show me just how special you are,' Jennifer told him. 'I said that I'd wasted too many years not knowing and that I was making up for lost time.'

'Come here,' Andrew ordered. 'I've got some making up to do myself.'

On Sunday, Andrew and Michael sent off to rugby in the pouring rain. When Andrew returned after the session in the pub with the other fathers he gave Jennifer a wry smile. 'Meet the temporary new coach for the midget team,' he said. 'Do you think we can find a pair of boots to fit Angus?'

'I think they just wear their gumboots to start with.' Jennifer grinned. 'Who roped you into that?'

'Robert Manson, that fire officer I met at the accident. Liam's dad was there as well. And Tom Bartlett. Tom's going to come by next week when the weather clears up and show me how to use a fence strainer. Mike and I are going to fix that fence at the back of the pond. Button's going to get out of that paddock if we don't do something about it.'

'Button's far too lazy to go anywhere by himself. He likes it right here.'

'So do I.' Andrew smiled.

Even Sonic the hedgehog was adding to the domestic contentment by appearing to thrive.

He now had powdered kitten-weaning formula mixed in with his milk. His eyes had opened and he got positively frisky in the evenings when he was allowed out of the shoebox to play. Soon he would graduate to eating tinned cat meat and they would have to start thinking about releasing him in the garden.

Angus was competing with Elvis for the position of Andrew's faithful shadow. If Michael was at all jealous, he hid it well. The treehouse took shape over the next week and, watching Andrew manoeuvre the large planks for the flooring high into the shadowy recesses of the ancient macrocarpa tree, Jennifer realised how much of his strength had now returned. Stripped to a T-shirt over his faded jeans, thanks to the warmth of the perfect afternoon weather, the firm shape of the muscles in Andrew's arms and shoulders was a pleasure to observe. The way the denim clung to the lean contours of his lower body was even more of a pleasure. Jennifer indulged herself until Andrew noticed her gaze.

'I think you're completely recovered,' Jennifer told him hurriedly. She hoped the children wouldn't notice her heightened colour. 'You're looking…good.'

Andrew adjusted his hold on the next plank. The detour that took him close to where Jennifer was standing was too casual to arouse the children's interest. Only Jennifer was aware of the contact of their hips as Andrew paused. And the tickle of his lips on her ear as he bent forward to speak very quietly.

'You, my love, look good enough to eat.' The deep rumble of Andrew's voice sent a shiver right down to Jennifer's toes.

'I don't know about you—' Andrew's tone was deceptively light as he returned to his task '—but I'm getting *very* hungry.'

The children were swift to agree but thoughts of dinner weren't yet registering with Jennifer. She had caught the blatant message in Andrew's glance as he moved away. This time her reaction was more than a pleasurable shiver. The sensual promise in those dark eyes was enough to melt her bones.

'Um… Me, too,' Jennifer managed. She stooped to extract Angus from the muddy puddle he had created for his plastic duck to swim in. 'I'll go and get things ready.'

'You do that.' Andrew's encouragement was as enthusiastic as his grin. 'Let me know if you need a hand.'

'I'll manage.' Jennifer hoped her voice didn't sound as strangled as it felt. 'Maybe I'll need your help later.'

'I'm sure you will.' Andrew sounded supremely confident. 'In fact, I'm counting on it.'

It became a habit for Andrew to drop into the hospital before collecting the children from school. Angus would vanish into the kitchen where Ruby delivered chocolate cake and cuddles. Andrew would spend time with Jennifer and Brian. His interest in the history of the small hospital had inspired Brian to dig out more and more old records and photographs. The older doctor was beginning to talk about collating them and writing up some sort of a book if he ever found the time. Jennifer relished the opportunity to discuss patients with Andrew. He might be a specialist surgeon but his general knowledge was impressive and he didn't seem to have forgotten much of what he'd learned at medical school. His practical skills were called on again the following Wednesday when Alice Hogan, the young farmer's wife whose pregnancy Jennifer had confirmed only weeks ago, was rushed in by her frantic husband.

Alice was pale, sweating and nauseous. 'I've got this terrible pain,' she told the doctors, and promptly collapsed in the corridor. It was Andrew who swept her up into his arms and carried her to the treatment room. And it was Andrew who diagnosed a ruptured ectopic pregnancy and confirmed Jennifer's suspicion that they were dealing with a major emergency.

'What's her gestation?'

'About twelve weeks.'

'What's the blood pressure?'

'Only 90 over 60.'

'Her abdomen's rigid. She's losing a lot of blood. How soon can we get her to a surgeon?'

'A helicopter can be here in twenty minutes. I'll call them now. Can you get an IV line in and start fluids?'

'Sure.'

'Change that acute oxygen mask for a non-rebreather,' Jennifer instructed Wendy. 'And get the monitor leads on.'

It was fortunate that the weather was fine enough for an evacuation by air. Jennifer and Andrew found themselves together again in the modified Land Rover that was the local ambulance, monitoring a critically ill patient as they waited for the helicopter to land on the rugby field. Mickey was driving again and took both doctors back to the hospital afterwards.

'Do you think she'll be OK?' he asked. 'She looked pretty sick.'

'She's shocked. She needs to get to Theatre quickly so they can stop the internal bleeding.'

'Shame you couldn't have done it here,' Mickey told Andrew. 'If we'd had another storm like the last one you might have had to.'

'I'm not an obstetrician,' Andrew responded. 'I wouldn't be happy tackling something like that.'

'But you could have if you'd had to,' Mickey persisted. 'Couldn't you?'

'I suppose so,' Andrew agreed. 'In a life-threatening emergency you have to try anything.'

'Like Liam's.' Mickey nodded. 'You saved him.' He eyed Andrew in the rear-view mirror. 'You're a bit of a hero around here, mate.'

A few days later Andrew Stephenson put the seal on his local reputation. The gathering of parents at the after-school pick-up time was now used to Andrew's presence and he was becoming accustomed to their sharing of personal information. While he would never consider divulging confidential patient details, he was happy to provide any general medical facts or explanations that were requested. The other parents all knew that Alice Hogan had lost her baby and that the chances of becoming pregnant again had diminished because of the surgery that had necessitated removal of one of her Fallopian tubes. The concern for a well-liked member of their small community had led to discussions about support for Alice and her husband in the future. It had been Andrew they had turned to, wanting to know about the medical possibilities for another baby. Alice's age and previous difficulty conceiving made IVF sound like the best option, and if funds were needed for the treatment they would all find some way to assist.

The group of parents were mostly female and included Susan Begg, whose oldest child had now started school. Susan had already confided the details of her recent hospital visit to her friends. She did have the condition of hypertrophic cardiomyopathy, where the heart muscle increased in weight and affected the flow of blood. The risk of a sudden cardiac death was present but Susan wasn't keen on the idea of an implantable cardiac defibrillator. She was now taking a drug that controlled the arrhythmias thought to be responsible for the sudden deaths associated with the condition. Andrew had heard the medical side of the story from Jennifer on one of his recent visits to the hospital.

'There's no evidence that the syncopal episodes are caused by a ventricular arrhythmia and an ICD is an invasive treatment,' Jennifer had told him. 'The cardiologists want to try amiodarone as a control medication and do some Holter monitoring on a regular basis. If there's a collapse that can be proved to be due to VT or VF then an implantable defibrillator will be the answer.'

'If she survives,' Andrew had added.

Susan would probably not have survived the VF cardiac arrest if she hadn't happened to suffer it while waiting to pick up her son from school. She was standing right beside Andrew, in fact, when it happened. The preschool children were all occupied in the adventure playground under the supervision of one of the mothers. The rest of the parents were occupied in an ordinary conversation about the upcoming pets' day at school. Susan suddenly stopped speaking. Her eyes rolled up and her eyelids fluttered. Andrew caught her as she collapsed and eased her to the ground.

'Susan!' He rubbed his knuckles on her sternum to provide a painful stimulus. 'Can you hear me?'

'My God,' one of the mothers gasped. 'What's happened to her?'

'Is it her heart?' someone else asked in a horrified whisper.

Andrew tilted Susan's head back to open her airway. He placed his cheek near her nose and mouth and rested a hand gently on her abdomen to feel as well as watch and listen for signs of respiration. There were none.

'Someone call the ambulance,' he ordered tersely. 'And call the hospital as well. Let Dr Tremaine know what's happening.'

Pinching Susan's nostrils closed, Andrew sealed his mouth over hers and inflated her lungs with a slow, deep breath. Then he repeated the action. His hand moved automatically to Susan's neck to feel for a carotid pulse. He could feel nothing. Just as automatically, Andrew swiftly ran his hand up the line of Susan's lower ribs until he reached the sternal notch. Two fingers' breadth up from the notch he placed the heel of his other hand. With the fingers of both hands then laced together, Andrew straightened his arms and began compressions, counting silently.

One of the group of women began to cry. Another put her arms around the weeping woman. The others stood, overwhelmed by the horror of the situation, waiting for instructions from Andrew who clearly knew exactly what he was doing. Andrew gave Susan another two breaths and continued the compressions.

'Does anyone here know how to do rescue breathing?'

'I did a first-aid course years ago,' Jill McIntosh responded. 'I'll try.'

'Good. Give her one breath for every five compressions,' Andrew instructed. 'Make sure you get a good seal around her mouth.'

Jill knelt beside Susan's head. She looked petrified.

'One, two, three, four, five,' Andrew counted aloud. 'OK—breathe.' He nodded a second later. 'That's great, Jill. I felt that breath going in. Three, four, five. Breathe again.'

They had established a practised rhythm by the time help arrived a few minutes later. Jennifer and Brian were first on the scene. Jennifer leapt from her car, deposited a life-pack beside Susan and uncurled the electrode wires with rapid movements. Brian carried a portable oxygen cylinder and bag mask. Jill moved out of the way to allow the doctors access.

'Go inside,' Andrew told Jill. 'Make sure the children don't get let out of school just yet.'

The ambulance arrived and Mickey joined the doctors.

'It's VF,' Jennifer confirmed, looking at the screen of the lifepack. 'Mickey, give Andrew a break with the compressions, would you? He must be getting exhausted.'

Andrew had forgotten how tiring CPR was and how hard it was on the knees to be kneeling on tarmac. He watched as Jennifer applied defibrillation pads to Susan's chest.

'I'll get an IV line in,' he suggested.

Jennifer nodded. 'That'd be great. OK, I'm charging up the paddles. Stand clear,' she ordered seconds later. Brian lifted the bag mask from Susan's face and moved back. 'I'm clear,' Jennifer stated. 'Everyone else clear?'

Affirmatives were quickly given. Susan's body jerked in response to the shock but it wasn't enough to jolt her heart back into a normal rhythm. Andrew quickly slipped the cannula into a vein in Susan's arm and taped it down. If defibrillation didn't work soon they would have to start giving drugs.

'Charging again,' Jennifer said calmly. 'Everybody clear.'

The second shock had the same result. 'Charging to 360,' Jennifer said quietly. 'Third time lucky.'

This time the shock worked. Susan's heart resumed a normal sinus rhythm and she began breathing on her own. Another minute and she began to regain consciousness, struggling to sit up.

'Stay still for a bit, Susan,' Jennifer said firmly.

'Why?' Susan's eyes opened and she gazed at the circle of faces above her in confusion. 'What's going on? What's all the fuss about?'

The children were coming out of school now and the crowd around Susan swelled considerably. Excited small voices alerted the adults to the approach of the helicopter. The hum of the rotors soon became louder. 'Look!'

the children shrieked. 'It's going to land on our *playground*!'

'Everybody stand right back here,' their teacher ordered loudly.

'What's the helicopter here for?' Susan sounded bewildered.

'You,' Jennifer told her. She gripped Susan's hand. 'You're going to be fine, Susan, but your heart went into just the sort of rhythm we were worried about. The sort that *can* lead to sudden death.' She smiled at her patient. 'It was very sensible of you to be standing beside a doctor when it happened. We've got things under control now but you need to be monitored in hospital.' Jennifer glanced at the long strip of ECG trace the lifepack was now printing out. 'And we've got proof of what happened. They'll want you to have an implantable defibrillator now to make sure it doesn't happen again.'

'You're telling me I almost died just now.' Susan was stunned. 'I think I'll be quite keen that it doesn't happen again, too.'

The children and parents all stayed to watch Susan being loaded into the helicopter.

Everybody was waving as it took off and hovered briefly before heading back towards Christchurch. Brian, however, wasn't watching. He was sitting inside Jennifer's vehicle as the helicopter disappeared over the hills.

Andrew was holding Angus by the hand as he came back from the playground. He paused by the car.

'You look dreadful, Brian. What's the matter?'

Jennifer was following him. She, too, looked at Brian's grey face with concern.

'I'm fine.' Brian waved his hand irritably. 'Let's get back to work.'

'You don't look fine,' Andrew stated.

'Leave it, Drew,' Jennifer advised quietly. 'I'll look after this.' She closed the passenger door and moved quickly to the driver's seat of her four-by-four. The sooner she got Brian back to the hospital the better. Susan's emergency had taken a toll and Brian's level of stress would only be exacerbated by Andrew's concern and public scrutiny. She knew that Andrew wouldn't be happy being shut out of the situation and Jennifer wasn't surprised when he turned up at the hospital an hour later.

'The children are at Sam's house,' he told Jennifer. 'Jill's happy to look after them. I want to know what's going on here. How's Brian?'

'He's OK. He's resting at home. Things are pretty well back to normal, thank goodness. And Susan's safely in the coronary care unit. They've got her booked for an ICD procedure tomorrow.'

'What's wrong with Brian?' Andrew shut the door of the office behind him.

'He's got coronary artery disease. He had an angioplasty two years ago and was fine until recently when he started getting unstable angina. He's been seen by a cardiologist and is on a waiting list for catheterisation and probable referral for repeat angioplasty or bypass grafting.'

'He's not in any condition to deal with emergencies.'

'He knows that. Fortunately we don't get too many of them.'

'You've had three in just over three weeks. Liam and Alice and now Susan. The stress of any case like that could have been disastrous. He shouldn't be here.'

'Do you want to be the one to tell him? It's not just a job we're talking about here, Andrew. Providing medical care in a small community becomes your life. Especially when you've been doing it for a very long time. It takes a special breed of person and Brian is one of the best. I've known him all my life. He persuaded me to stay on here and I haven't regretted it. He's an inspiration both on a personal and a professional front and I need him. This practice and hospital is too big for one doctor to manage.'

'So get another partner. A third doctor.'

'We'll have to.' Jennifer nodded. 'But the suggestion has to come from Brian, not me. He knows it's inevitable. He just needs time to accept it and I'm not going to push him.'

'And in the meantime you get saddled with an increasing workload and the worry that you might not be available to deal with every emergency that comes along.'

'I'll cope.'

'You don't have to. Not alone, anyway. I could help.'

'You don't have a practising certificate. You're not trained as a GP.'

'Maybe I can do something about that.'

'If you've lost your licence in the States you won't be able to get a certificate here.'

'Maybe I haven't. I've been out of contact for more than six months. Maybe it's time I found out exactly where I stand so that I can do something about moving forward with my life. I want to practise medicine again, Jennifer. You were right. You don't give up being a doctor just because you lose your job.'

'You want to move forward *here*? As a rural GP?'

'Why not?'

'You're a specialist surgeon.'

'I had exactly the same training you did. Sure, I might need some retraining in some areas. Are you accredited to take on a trainee GP here?'

'Kind of. Brian trained me and he was the best teacher I could have had. I attended courses in Christchurch and sat the exams in Wellington, but he's never talked about taking on another trainee.'

'Maybe that's the perfect way to give him time to ease out of his position. He can watch over my shoulder and I can do all the work. He could find time to write up the history of the hospital as well.'

'But why? What's the attraction for you? You're a surgeon. If you can practise in New Zealand, why not go for a job at a main centre, like Christchurch?'

'Maybe being a surgeon isn't what I really wanted. Been there, done that. And maybe I don't want to be that far away. From you.'

'You'd give up surgery? To be with me?'

'I wouldn't give it up entirely. We could get a theatre up and running for minor procedures and emergencies. You could do some more training in anaesthetics. We'd be partners.'

Jennifer's breath caught. 'I would never have imagined you as a GP. Not in a million years.'

'Maybe coming here has taught me that medicine has more to offer than I'd realised.

Like being part of a community—a way to belong somewhere. Something I've never had. And, more importantly, I could be part of a family. *Our* family, Jen. I want to marry you and have children. Our own children. Another generation that will know just how firmly they belong. Family history in the most beautiful place on earth. Parents that love them as much as they love each other.'

'I do love you, Drew.' Jennifer reached out to touch his face. 'So much.'

'So, do you think you could cope with some more children? It doesn't have to be straight away.' Andrew was smiling as he drew Jennifer close. 'We could get married first.' He bent his head to place a tender kiss on Jennifer's lips. And then another.

'I could cope.' Jennifer managed to draw breath briefly. 'I can't think of anything I'd rather cope with.'

Andrew paused before the next kiss. 'So you'll marry me?'

'Yes.' Jennifer was smiling through threatened tears. Andrew caught a glistening drop on her lower lashes with his thumb.

'You don't look very happy about it.'

'Oh, I'm happy,' Jennifer assured him. 'I've never been happier.' She blinked hard and smiled again. 'Can you imagine how excited the twins will be at the prospect of being bridesmaids?'

'Michael could be best man. And Angus could carry the rings.'

'And we could have flower dogs.' Jennifer was laughing now. 'What a circus!'

'I can't wait,' Andrew told her.

'Neither can I.'

CHAPTER EIGHT

IT WAS too good to be true. Too perfect to last.

For three days, Jennifer walked on air and basked in the bliss of imagining a future that was all she could have ever wished for. The engagement was kept unofficial—a secret that was shared by only two people and discussed in whispers in the aftermath of love-making that was as tender as it was passionate. Everyone knew something was happening and adults exchanged knowing glances and satisfied smiles. The children had already accepted Andrew as part of their lives. If he and Jennifer were going to spend their time staring at each other and smiling a lot then that was fine by them.

Andrew dug out his address book from one of his boxes and used the e-mail connection on the hospital computing system to contact his solicitor and ex-colleagues in the States. As soon as he knew how things stood he could make plans for his professional future and put them into action. Neither he nor Jennifer wanted to wait and yet the anticipation of progress was surely as delightful as any success could hope to be.

The only problem with e-mail was that it wasn't necessarily as private as the recipient might have preferred. The response to Andrew's communication came in a wave of e-mails that initially confused Brian. He called Andrew into the office the next afternoon as soon as Angus had been left in the kitchen for his visit with Ruby. Jennifer, passing the men in the hallway, took one look at Brian's face and followed them.

'I wasn't being nosy,' Brian said apologetically to Andrew. 'I couldn't figure out why we were being contacted by an American law firm. I had the horrible thought we might be being sued by some tourist we treated last summer. It wasn't until I was halfway through that I realised what it was about.'

Andrew was rapidly scanning the printout he held.

'I had no idea.' Brian shook his head sadly. 'But I'm glad it was me that caught the mail. Normally, it's Judith, our secretary, that prints out things in the mornings. You wouldn't want something like this to become common knowledge, I'm sure.' Brian still looked uncomfortable. 'I can assure you that no one will hear a word about it from me and I've deleted it from the computer.'

Jennifer looked pale. Was this the formal notification of the aftermath a malpractice suit could result in? A written confirmation that his licence had been revoked? A statement to the effect that Andrew Stephenson would never practise medicine again?

'What is it, Drew?' Her words were agonised. 'What do they say?'

Andrew handed her the sheet of paper in silence. Jennifer read so quickly she thought she had misinterpreted the words. She tried again. 'But this is good news,' she said in surprise. 'You've been cleared of any charges.'

'And William Chadwick has been sued.' Andrew whistled softly. 'His problems with alcohol and drug misuse obviously became impossible to cover up. At least the rest of the team stood together and refused to give him the opportunity to kill someone else.'

'And they've vindicated you. Oh, Drew, I'm so pleased for you!'

'Better late than never, I guess.' Andrew grinned. He turned to Brian. 'It's a long story but I'd better fill you in. Got time for a coffee?'

The older doctor smiled. 'Of course.'

'This means there's no barrier for you getting registration here,' Jennifer exclaimed. 'You can do whatever you want.'

'Sure can.' Andrew still looked stunned. 'Calls for a bottle of champagne, I reckon. This needs celebrating.'

Brian looked from Jennifer to Andrew and back again. 'We've got some world-class restaurants tucked away in these parts, Drew. Perfect for celebrations. I'll bet you haven't tried any of them yet.'

Andrew grinned. 'Do they cater for children? And maybe a dog or two?'

Brian smiled. 'I think Pat and I could well be available for a spot of babysitting tonight.

Pat's been complaining she hasn't seen the children recently. Why don't you two go and have a nice dinner and an even nicer bottle of champagne?'

Andrew winked at Jennifer. 'Sounds like a plan. Thanks, Brian.'

'My pleasure.' Brian placed a hand on Andrew's shoulder. 'But you owe me a coffee. And a story. Let's go and visit Ruby.'

The e-mails that arrived the next day were more personal. They may not have had an accent but they all sounded very American. Where on the face of the earth had Drew been hiding himself? The team at the private hospital in Boston had been desperate to contact him for the last two months. Wasn't the news fantastic? The lawsuit for reparation they had instigated on his behalf would make him a millionaire—at least. He had to come back. They were desperate to have him. He could not only rejoin the team—but lead it.

Jennifer read the effusive correspondence with increasing trepidation. 'These offers are amazing, Drew. Do you want to go back?'

'I'll have to. At least for a while. There are legalities to settle and some personal loose ends to tie up. It might take a few weeks. Come with me, Jen.' Andrew's smile was engaging. 'The States wouldn't be a bad place for a honeymoon.'

Andrew came in early to the hospital the next day. He wanted to spend time on the Internet looking at airline schedules and ticket availability. And he couldn't wait to check the e-mails.

'This is fantastic!' He waved a sheet of paper at Jennifer when she entered the office with Angus trotting at her heels. 'The new research programmes they've got up and running are rather exciting. Some of them are based on work I started before I left. Just listen to this…'

But Jennifer didn't have time to listen. 'Can you keep Angus in here, please? He's driving Ruby mad, banging pots in the kitchen, and I have an antenatal patient waiting and a well-child clinic to run in fifteen minutes.'

Andrew's enthusiasm waned visibly. 'Aren't you interested?'

'Of course I'm interested. I just have other things to think about right now. Melissa Cooper is eight months pregnant and her blood pressure is going up. Research projects on the other side of the globe will just have to wait. Tell me later.'

Andrew did tell her later. He was still talking about it late that night as they prepared for bed. 'There's a conference in a few weeks where a lot of the data is going to be presented. *My* data. They want me to give a presentation. In Miami. It'll be a huge conference.'

'Are you going to go, then?'

'*We* could go. You'd love it. Interesting place, interesting people to meet.'

'Part of the honeymoon?' Jennifer asked drily. She had been watching Andrew's enthusiasm growing ever since the first e-mail from his old colleagues. Was he unaware of the looming showdown? Jennifer was trying to ignore it. She was trying to pretend that what was being offered to Andrew a world away wasn't going to be enough to take him away for good. After all, he was assuming that she would be with him. Did it not occur to Andrew how impossible it would be for her to leave for more than a few days? A honeymoon could be arranged—with difficulty. But it had been a planned honeymoon that had brought Andrew to Akaroa and it hadn't taken long for him to decide that it could be a permanent arrangement. Now he was planning another honeymoon.

Andrew looked contrite. 'I'm sorry, Jen. Sorting out my legal hassles and going to a conference wouldn't be much of a honeymoon, would it? It's just that the opportunities are so exciting. I feel like I've been let out of jail or something.' He reached for Jennifer and held her close. 'It doesn't change how I feel about you. It can't affect *us*.'

But it could. And did. Andrew's campaign to persuade Jennifer that the world was their oyster was anything but subtle. Michael started looked sulky and withdrawn again.

'Why does Drew keep talking about America? I thought he liked being here. I thought he liked *us*.'

'He does.' Jennifer tried to sound more convinced than she felt herself. 'Of course he does. Hey, are you still going to sleep up in the treehouse if it's fine this weekend?'

'No.' Michael's tone was belligerent. 'It's a stupid treehouse.'

The twins were squabbling more often in their efforts to attract Andrew's attention and Angus had thrown his first full-blown tantrum when Zippy chewed up his treasured yellow plastic duck. Worse still came the next day when the baby hedgehog was found dead in the shoebox by the twins at his after-school feeding time.

'It's Mike's fault,' Jessica said accusingly. 'He forgot to feed Sonic his breakfast.'

'I did not! He just didn't want to eat it.'

'He must have been sick,' Jennifer said sadly. 'I'm sorry.'

'You should have given him some medicine.' Sophie stared at Jennifer as tears gathered.

'I'm sorry,' Jennifer repeated. 'If I could have done something, I would have.' She put the lid on the shoebox. 'We'll have to bury him.'

'No-o-o-o!' Sophie and Jessica wailed in unison.

Michael kicked at something imaginary on the carpet. 'I don't care,' he announced loudly. 'It was a stupid hedgehog.'

'He was *not*!' Sophie aimed a kick at Michael.

'Come on.' Jennifer stood up, holding the box. 'I'll dig the hole. Maybe you girls could find some flowers.'

Jessica's tears flowed harder. 'Can we pick the new daffodils?'

'Sure.' Jennifer looked at Michael. 'Do you want to help us, Mike?'

'No.'

In the end, Jennifer was left to bury Sonic by herself. Distracted by picking enough flowers for a suitable tribute, the girls vanished into the outskirts of the garden. Michael had shut himself in his bedroom and Angus was in the kitchen with Andrew. Funny how it had been Andrew who had been delegated the responsibility of Sonic's health check on arrival but it was Jennifer who carried the can for not providing lifesaving medication to stave off his departure.

Andrew was suitably sympathetic to the twins' grief at dinnertime but he was clearly preoccupied. Jennifer doubted that he even noticed how withdrawn Michael was. She couldn't lay any blame for Sonic's demise at Andrew's feet but the general atmosphere of uncertainty and tension in the house had a very obvious source. It was all brewing up into some form of a confrontation and by late that evening Jennifer knew the flash point had been reached.

Andrew had booked tickets to Boston. One-way tickets for a flight leaving in three days' time. He waited until the children were all in bed before showing Jennifer.

'They were the only seats I could get for the next fortnight. There's a court hearing for the lawsuit on my behalf next week. I really ought to be there for that.'

'And when are you planning to come back?'

'I'm not sure. Let's see how things pan out when we get there. You might really like Boston.'

'It wouldn't matter if I liked it or not. I can't just drop things here and take off, Andrew. Even for a few days. Who would look after the children?'

'Saskia would come back if you asked her.'

'She's seventeen! I wouldn't leave her with sole responsibility for everything. It's far too much to ask.'

'You've got a whole community out there that would help out if you asked.'

'This is *my* family,' Jennifer reminded him.

'What about the children's father, then? He's coming for a visit soon. Get him to come earlier.'

'I can't do that. Anyway, I've got a job here. A full-time position.'

'You've got a partner. Brian can hold the fort just for a few days.'

'No, he can't. I wouldn't even ask and you know why.'

'Get a locum, then. You were going to get a third doctor here.'

'You were going to *be* the third doctor here. Or have you forgotten?'

'No, I hadn't forgotten.' Andrew had gone from looking frustrated to clearly angry. He took a deep breath. 'It's just that things have changed, Jen. There's more to think about and I've been doing a lot of thinking.'

'And you think that maybe you would like your old job back.' Jennifer's suggestion was calm but her heart was thumping erratically. 'The one with all the money and prestige.'

'No, it's not like that. Can't you see what's being offered to us? *Us*—not just me.'

'I'm not going to go and live in Boston, Andrew. I can't.'

'And I can't stay here. Not yet, anyway.'

Jennifer felt a chill. A sensation of dread combined with a feeling of inevitability. This had had to come. And here it was.

'You want me to send the children back to their father and go to Boston with you.'

'Don't get me wrong here,' Andrew said quietly. 'I know how much you love these kids. I love them, too. But they're not *our* children. They *should* be with their father.'

'They will be. When he's ready.'

'You're so prepared to sacrifice what you want or need for other people, Jen. What about me? What about you? Why can't you do what *you* want?'

'I am doing what I want.'

'I thought you wanted to be with me. For the rest of your life.'

'I do.' Jennifer fought back tears. 'I don't believe this. You sound just like Hamish.'

'Maybe he was right.' Andrew was staring at Jennifer as though seeing her for the first time. He sounded impatient. 'You've already sacrificed your ambitions once for the sake of your family. Don't do it again.' His tone mellowed. 'Come with me, Jen. You could retrain and become a surgeon. Try the excitement of working in a huge American hospital. Dramatic life and death case load. Every day!'

Jennifer shook her head sharply. 'I don't have those ambitions any more. I only had to live and work here for long enough to realise how empty they were. You said yourself that being a famous surgeon wasn't all it was cracked up to be. That it wasn't what you really wanted.'

Andrew shrugged and looked away. 'I was bitter about being forced out. Being blamed for something I didn't do. And maybe I felt I deserved part of the blame. I could have stopped that operation. Or at least made a genuine protest by walking out. Maybe I would have saved that woman's life.'

'That woman! I'll bet you can't even remember her name.' Jennifer's scathing words tumbled out too quickly for Andrew to interrupt or contradict her. 'And even if you can, you wouldn't have a clue what her childhood illnesses were or what her family circumstances were really like.' Jennifer snorted with contempt. 'So much for your statement that practising medicine had more to offer than just rearranging unconscious people and sending them on their way. So much for wanting to be part of a community.' Jennifer shook her head sadly. 'I wonder how much else you said was simply hot air. Like how you felt about me.'

'Are you saying you don't trust me now?'

Jennifer shrugged. 'I believed what you told me. Maybe I got carried away by your rosy scenario of us working together as partners.

Building up the hospital facilities and working as a team to provide this community with something to be proud of. Maybe I just wanted to believe it too much. It's the kind of professional ambition I dream about these days. The only kind.'

'I'm not saying it isn't worthwhile. We wouldn't have to forget about it. Just postpone it.'

'Nice retirement job? Nothing too stressful or challenging... Or dynamic? Retire to the country and potter about, being a GP?'

'*No.*' Andrew was pacing now, clearly upset. He stopped and turned abruptly. 'Look, all I'm saying is that if things had gone differently, it wouldn't have been my first choice for a career.'

'Of course not,' Jennifer agreed. 'You can't know what you're missing if you've never been exposed to it. You have to experience something to know it's what you really want. Living and working here wasn't my first choice either, but—'

'Exactly,' Andrew interrupted. 'But you stayed because you loved it and because you didn't have anything you'd left behind that really mattered. I left my reputation. My self-esteem. Sure, I could stay and be happy but I would always have that huge black blot on my copybook. The knowledge that people believed I wasn't good enough. That I wasn't worth supporting. Just the sort of emotional baggage my childhood left me with. I have to go back. To prove them wrong. To prove to myself that I can believe they really want me.'

'And are they the people that really matter?'

'Of course not. You're the person that really matters. That's why you have to come with me. I can show you what I'm really capable of achieving.'

'I know what you're capable of. I've seen you work. *I* believed in you with no other evidence than your word. I don't need to go to the States. You don't have to prove anything except...' Jennifer stopped suddenly as a new thought intruded. A horrible thought.

'Except what?' Andrew asked coldly.

'You came here in the wake of a professional disaster. You've already admitted that working here wouldn't have been your first choice. It was available and you thought you could make the best of it and be reasonably happy.' Jennifer took a deep, slow breath. 'You also came here in the wake of a personal disaster. This trip was supposed to be your honeymoon, for heaven's sake. Maybe *I* was just available as well and you thought you should make the best of a limited choice.'

'You don't believe that.'

'I don't know what to believe any more, Andrew. As far as I can see, this is history repeating itself. My relationship with Hamish broke up because of my commitment to my family.'

'You didn't love Hamish. Not enough to want to make it work, anyway. Maybe that's the problem. Maybe you don't love me enough either.'

'My ties here are part of who I am. If I'm only acceptable without them then I'm not really wanted for myself. And that's not good enough.'

'What are you trying to say here, Jennifer?'

Jennifer's heart was breaking. 'I'm saying that I don't think this is the right place for you.

And I'm not the right woman. You have to know what you want and you have to be sure. Being here isn't your first choice—you said so yourself. And it's not enough to compete with a better offer. I think that speaks for itself.'

'It doesn't have to compete. I'm trying to find a compromise here. A relationship isn't going to work if one person makes the rules and refuses to try and understand what the other person needs.'

'Exactly.' Jennifer was keeping her self-control with difficulty. 'And ours isn't going to work. I can't leave.'

'And I can't stay.'

'Then go,' Jennifer said tightly. 'And go now. I don't think you have any idea the effect you're having on this family right now. The children don't know which way the wind is blowing and I'm not going to have them upset any more. And I'm not going to let this happen again. Not ever.'

'What's that supposed to mean?'

'I mean that if you go, that's it. You will have made your choice.'

'You're issuing an ultimatum. You're being selfish.'

'I'm protecting what I care about. Yes, I'm protecting myself as well.'

'So that's it? You're prepared to just let me walk away? I thought you loved me.'

'I did. I do. It's you that's doing the walking.'

'I *have* to.' Andrew's words were cold. Final.

'Fine.' Jennifer turned her back and headed for the door. 'Just don't come back.'

CHAPTER NINE

THE weeds in Brian's vegetable garden had already won the war.

Even last season's silverbeet clumps were barely distinguishable. The older doctor shook his head with resignation. Maybe in a few months' time he would be able to fork it over and start again, but there weren't going to be any fresh peas for Christmas dinner this year. His frustration was edged with a fear that he didn't want to confront. The distraction of a car pulling up at the front gate was welcome. The delight with which Brian greeted his visitors was genuine.

'Philip! It's about time you came to see us. You've been back for a week now, haven't you?'

Jennifer's brother-in-law shook Brian's hand warmly. 'I'm sorry, Brian. It's been hectic.'

Brian's wife, Pat, came bustling down the pathway, her apron flapping. She kissed Philip and welcomed him home, but her attention was quickly drawn to the small boy climbing out of the car.

'Angus! I'm making biscuits, my love. Do you want to come and help? Then we can find some flowers to pick in the garden for your aunty Jen.'

'They'll be lucky to find any flowers under those weeds,' Brian muttered as the men were left by the gate. 'The garden's a mess and I'm in no shape to do anything much about it.'

'Jen told me,' Philip said sympathetically. 'I'm sorry to hear about the problems you're having, Brian. She seems confident that the surgery will be a success, though. You're due to go into hospital later this month, aren't you?'

Brian nodded. 'Triple bypass. I'll be out of action for a while. I just hope we get some response to our advertisement for another doctor or Jennifer will have a lot to cope with.' He paused and frowned. 'How does she seem to you at the moment?'

'Quiet,' Philip said promptly. 'In fact, that's one of the reasons I came by this morning. I'm a bit worried about her.'

By tacit consent, the two men moved towards a garden bench. Warm sunshine and the subtle perfume from a mass of nearby daffodils enveloped them as they sat down.

'Gorgeous day,' Philip commented. 'But it's funny—this place doesn't feel like home any more. I just love the Gold Coast in Australia.'

'How are things going?'

'Brilliantly. The business has taken off and I've bought a house.' Philip's glance at his former GP was almost shy. 'I've met someone as well. I'm not rushing anything but she's a bit special.'

'I'm so pleased to hear that, Philip.' He eyed the younger man cautiously. 'Sounds like you're planning to make your move permanent.'

Philip nodded. 'I haven't told Jen yet but I'm ready to take the kids home. They're already dead keen to visit the Gold Coast since I told them about all the amusement parks.'

'It would be a big change for them.'

'I know. But this week has been brilliant, Brian. I hadn't realised just how much I've missed them all. The twins say they're never going to let me disappear again. It's been a real job getting them to go off to school in the mornings. I'm getting to know Angus properly for the first time as well. It's not a good thing to have a son you haven't watched grow from a baby into a boy.'

'Could you cope with them all on your own? Looking after four children and running a business won't be easy.'

'I'll have help. Anne can't wait to meet them. She can't have her own children because of a hysterectomy years ago after a disastrous pregnancy. I think the kids will love her but, as I say, I'm not rushing things. That's why I came on my own this time. I was going to leave suggesting that they come to live with me until my next visit at Christmas, but I don't want to wait any more and I can't just leave the kids again. I'm worried about how Jen might take it, though.'

'It will certainly change her life. The house will be very empty.'

'I was really hoping that something had developed with that chap she had staying. When I rang a few weeks ago it sounded like she'd found the man of her dreams. Even the kids couldn't stop telling me how wonderful Drew was. I felt quite jealous. But there's no sign of him now and Jennifer won't talk about him. Do you know what happened?'

'He left rather suddenly. He had to go back to the States for some unfinished business.'

'Was there anything serious going on between him and Jennifer?'

Brian smiled sadly. 'Oh, yes. You couldn't miss the atmosphere. They must have had a major falling out, I'd say. Jennifer looked dreadful for about a week after he left but, then, she was having some hassles finding child care and so forth. Drew had been looking after things since Saskia went home.'

'Maybe she'll be relieved when I take the children. It will make her life a lot less complicated. She might be able to sort things out with this Drew and make a new start for herself.'

'Maybe.' Brian looked unconvinced. 'When I tried to talk to her about him she clammed up. Said it was over. She'd made her choice and so had he.'

'I don't think she's very happy. Maybe she made the wrong choice.'

'Maybe,' Brian conceded. 'But that's something she'll have to work out for herself. She's as stubborn as her mother ever was and won't admit to anything in a hurry. The more miserable she is, the more determined she becomes to cope. By herself. Come on.' Brian eased himself to his feet. 'Let's go and see what those biscuits Pat and Angus are making taste like.'

Jennifer could cope. She was coping and she was quite confident that nobody knew how miserable she was. Having total chaos around her both at home and at the hospital was a definite bonus. If she seemed a little distracted or short-tempered at times, there were any number of extraneous circumstances to attribute a cause to.

A dozen crates littered the farmhouse, being packed with clothes, games, books and toys. The children were so excited about going to live with their father in Australia. Even Angus, who didn't understand any of the confusion and barely knew his father, was happiest when he was close to Philip. Michael seemed to have grown inches taller overnight. His dad was very impressed by the treehouse and the project on pollution and what Michael seemed to know about computers. They were going to buy a computer of his own, duty free, on their way out of the country.

Passports had to be rushed through for the children and arrangements made for Zippy to travel with them. He was Michael's dog now after all, and couldn't be left behind. Philip was even prepared to pay for the black kitten to move as well, after the twins had insisted she was part of the family. Jennifer would still have Tigger and Elvis, wouldn't she? That would be enough. Philip drew the line at exporting Button, the pony, however. They didn't have space at the new house. They would come back often to visit and the children could ride Button then. The next visit was only as far away as Christmas and they could count that in a matter of weeks. The compromise was only reached after much argument by the twins but the lure of being with their father permanently was enough to win the day.

'You'll look after Button, won't you, Jen? He won't forget us, will he?'

Jennifer had tried to smile and sound reassuring. She was trying to share the children's happiness and not feel as though she was about to be abandoned, having served her purpose as a temporary parent. Trying not to feel jealous of the woman Philip couldn't help talking about. The 'Anne' that this group of affectionate children would probably accept and love in no time flat. Trying not to think that she might have lost her only chance at what Philip had to look forward to. A future with his own children and a partner.

There was no real relief from an atmosphere of excited anticipation at work either. Liam was being transferred from Christchurch hospital to recuperate at Akaroa hospital before returning home. A group of locals had decided to welcome him in style and a party was being prepared, along with the best room the hospital had to offer. Ruby was reigning supreme in the kitchens, organising an afternoon tea for an expected crowd of fifty people. Balloons and flowers were being arranged in Liam's room and his father was up a ladder by the front door attaching the 'Welcome Home' banner that Liam's siblings had painted.

Jennifer was managing to work through all this. She was coping perfectly well. Maybe it helped that she wasn't touched by the excitement of any of it. She could concentrate on the practical and get everything that needed to be done sorted out without being distracted by endless reminiscences about the past or hopeful discussions of the joys the future promised.

She'd had more than her share of dreams recently. Dreams that had come crashing down around her ears and left her this huge emptiness inside. A void that was going to have to be filled with whatever Jennifer could find to throw in. It wasn't going to be hard to find enough to work on. While it would never be possible to fill that void completely, if she worked hard enough she could build a wall around it and then a lid. She could cover it over and forget about it and simply get on with the rest of her life.

What made it more difficult, almost unbearable, was that no matter what Jennifer did she found reminders of Andrew. How had he managed to infiltrate every aspect of her life to such an extent in such a short time? Even what should have been a minor emergency case arriving at the hospital that morning had eventually drawn Jennifer's thoughts towards Andrew. The unexpected appointment had proved frustrating and Jennifer had excused herself from the consulting room in the hope that Brian might be able to offer guidance. Brian was in the office, attending to the mail. Wendy was also there, having just delivered morning tea to the senior doctor.

'I've got Freda Scott in the consulting room,' Jennifer told them. 'She tripped over in the garden yesterday and her right wrist is painful and swollen with restricted movement. There's no obvious fracture but I've told her she needs to go to Christchurch for an X-ray.

She's flatly refused. She says if she can't walk, she's not going anywhere.'

Brian was clearly not surprised. 'I don't think Freda's been in a vehicle for ten years.'

Wendy's head was tilted thoughtfully. 'Doesn't Freda live in that tiny cottage on Rue Balguerie? With about twelve cats? I've heard she's a little odd.'

Brian smiled tolerantly. 'Freda moved here about thirty years ago and ran a small drapery shop. She's always been on her own and very independent. She never goes near a doctor by choice. I've only ever seen her once as a patient and that was after a car accident nearly twenty years ago. She knocked over young Stewart Maloney when he ran out in front of her car.'

'I remember that accident,' Jennifer exclaimed. 'Stewart was in my class. Some police officer came and gave the whole school a talking to about road safety. Stewart wasn't badly hurt.'

'He got knocked out,' Brian said. 'Freda thought she'd killed him and swore she'd never get behind a wheel again. She hasn't. I suspect she's developed a phobia about other people driving as well. I've heard that she takes down the number plates of all cars she thinks are breaking the speed limit and reports them to Tom Bartlett. She's been known to issue a ticket or two herself.'

Wendy was grinning but Jennifer shook her head. 'No wonder she's so adamant about not going to Christchurch. Maybe I should organise an ambulance transfer.' She chewed her lip. 'It could be just a bad sprain. If we had X-ray facilities here we could manage this sort of case without having to send them anywhere.' Jennifer tried to ignore the unbidden memory of Andrew's ambition to build up the hospital facilities, but it was impossible. She wished she hadn't said anything.

'Why can't we get X-rays here?' Wendy mused.

'Too expensive,' Brian responded. 'And we'd need someone trained to use the equipment.'

'It can't be too difficult to get trained,' Jennifer pointed out. 'The nurse at the veterinary clinic does them.'

'That's it!' Wendy chuckled. 'Take Freda to the vet.'

'It's more the reading of results that needs expertise,' Brian commented. 'Some fractures are hard to pick up but the outcome can be poor if they're treated appropriately.'

'I could get training,' Jennifer said decisively. 'We'd be able to handle a lot of cases ourselves. Anything that was tricky could still be referred.'

'What about the cost? Our budget would never cope.'

'We could raise the money. Get community support. Look at all the people we've got coming in to welcome Liam this morning. Let's talk about a fundraising campaign to buy our own X-ray machine while they're here.'

Brian was smiling. 'You're keen on this idea, aren't you, Jen? Have you got any idea how much time and work it would involve?'

Jennifer straightened her back. 'Maybe a project like this is just what I need. I'm going to have a lot more time available when the children go to Australia.' She nodded with satisfaction as a solution to a more immediate concern presented itself. 'I could get the ambulance that brings Liam to take Freda back to town. You come and talk to her, Brian. I'm sure she'll listen to you.'

Jennifer led the way, feeling cautiously optimistic about more than her patient's management. She didn't need Andrew Stephenson's ideas or support to achieve results. She waited for Brian to catch her up in the hallway. 'When we interview the applicants for the new partner's position, let's try and find somebody with a strong interest in minor surgery. There's a lot more we could do here, you know.'

'If you're not careful, this place will take over your life completely, Jen.'

'It is my life,' Jennifer responded quietly. 'And I'm going to makc it something to be proud of.'

The community enthusiasm for fundraising was already something to be proud of. So was the depth of caring displayed by the welcome Liam Bellamy received at the small hospital. Jennifer was close to tears as she participated in the celebration. She was lucky to be part of it all. Where else could she be and gain this kind of depth and real involvement with others through her work? It certainly wouldn't come through a position at any large hospital. Especially in a foreign country. It really wasn't Jennifer's fault that her thoughts were again centering on Andrew. There wasn't one person present in this gathering that hadn't mentioned him. Wasn't it lucky that he'd been here on the night Liam had his accident? And isn't it a shame he's not here to enjoy the party? Even Liam wanted to talk about Andrew.

'I'd like to thank him,' he told Jennifer. 'Have you got his address? Maybe I could write him a letter.'

'I'm sure I can find out for you,' Jennifer said. 'What's this I hear from your dad about a career choice? Are you still keen on the idea of nursing?'

'No.' Liam grinned. 'I've changed my mind. I'm going to become a physiotherapist. Do you think I could come and work here?'

'Maybe one day.' Jennifer smiled. 'With the plans I've got for this place we could well be needing to expand our services.'

*   *   *

The frequent reminders of Andrew were even more poignant at home. The twins had to tell their father about Sonic the hedgehog and how Drew had stayed up *all* night to feed him with the eyedropper. Michael wanted a stir-fry meal for dinner on their last night together and even Elvis couldn't hope to fill the gap on the other side of Jennifer's bed. The flurry of the final departure was filled with such excitement from the children that Jennifer was able to ignore the reality of what she was now facing. She travelled into Christchurch to see them off and it was on the drive back to Akaroa that it finally hit home.

The house would be empty when she arrived home. Elvis would be waiting by the front door, but that was the only normality she could expect. That door would be closed. The house would be deserted and probably feel twice as huge as it was. Unless she was called out to a patient there would be no one to talk to. No company and no distractions. Maybe Michael had been right. It was stupid not having a television.

*   *   *

Andrew had been gone for over three weeks. He wasn't coming back. Jennifer had told him not to and they'd both been so angry and hurt when he'd left that she wasn't surprised he hadn't called. Jennifer's anger had faded rapidly. The hurt had taken longer. The emptiness of the house and the long quiet hours alone had given Jennifer a lot of time to think. She couldn't really blame Andrew. Her reasons for being here had evaporated. The final application date for the position as a partner in the practice was drawing close. Soon there would be medical cover for the community that would replace Brian and could cover for herself. If one new doctor was going to work here, why not two? One of the applications had come from a married team of two doctors who were planning to job share. Maybe it would naturally develop into two jobs.

If Jennifer had only known what had been about to transpire in the lives of her nieces and nephews, things would have gone very differently. What was holding her here now? The community and the level of involvement she felt in cases such as Liam's? Was it enough? More important than her love for Andrew?

No. As much as Jennifer loved her home and her work, she would give them up for this man. She needed to be with him no matter where it was. Maybe Boston wouldn't be her first choice but it didn't have to be for ever. The way she felt about Andrew was going to be for ever. Jennifer agonised over what she should do. Was it possible he could still feel the same way or had she destroyed that possibility? The more she thought about the way they'd parted the more Jennifer blamed herself. She could understand Andrew's need to return to Boston to experience vindication and reinstatement. Andrew had never been put first, not even as a child, and Jennifer had provided more of the same kind of rejection. She had made her work and responsibilities seem more important to her than he was. No wonder he had made no attempt to contact her since. It was up to her to put things right—if she still could. She had to try.

Directory enquiries was helpful in supplying the telephone number for the J.J. Shuster

Institute in Boston. They were seventeen hours behind New Zealand time so Jennifer calculated that to ring midmorning, she would need to stay up until three a.m. Given her unsatisfactory attempts to sleep at present, it wasn't difficult to stay awake. Nerves kicked in around midnight, however. What would she say? How would Andrew react?

Jennifer paced around the vast, empty house. Elvis became increasingly disconcerted by this unusual behaviour. With a resigned expression the shaggy black dog finally gave up his warm spot on the couch and followed Jennifer. He sat down hopefully every time she paused, wagging his plumed tail as encouragement, but his mistress seemed oblivious to his persuasive efforts. When Jennifer eventually picked up the telephone and sat down on the couch, Elvis climbed up and flopped beside her with a relieved grunt. He was rewarded with a hug.

'I'll just tell him the truth,' Jennifer told her dog. 'That I miss him. That I want to be with him. What's the worst that could happen?

Even if he tells me it's over I won't be any worse off than I am now.'

Except that she would be much worse off. The decision to ring Andrew had been made with the desperate need to find what had been lost. If it wasn't there to be found any more then Jennifer knew she would lose much more than just a relationship. She would lose the only future she wanted. Her fingers were trembling as she punched in the long international and area codes followed by the hospital number.

The call was answered quickly, by a young female with a strong southern accent.

'I'd like to speak to Dr Andrew Stephenson, please,' Jennifer said breathlessly.

'I beg your pardon? Could you repeat that, please?'

Jennifer repeated her request, more firmly this time. There was a moment's silence. 'I'm sorry but I'm not familiar with the name. Which department do you require?'

'Surgery. He's a surgeon.'

'Just one moment.' Music wafted over the phone line and Jennifer found herself listening to the old country and western song 'Tie a Yellow Ribbon Round the Old Oak Tree'. It seemed appropriate enough to make her throat constrict painfully. The song was cut off abruptly.

'I'm sorry, but Dr Stephenson is unavailable. He hasn't worked here for nearly a year.'

'He's come back,' Jennifer told her. 'Just recently.'

'Is that right? Hold the line, please.'

This time Jennifer got three verses and every chorus of 'Yellow Ribbon'. The new voice on the phone informed her that she had been transferred to the department of surgery.

'I'm trying to locate Dr Andrew Stephenson. I believe he returned to Boston a few weeks ago and is due to start work again at your hospital.'

The secretary she was now speaking to was more helpful. At least she had heard of Andrew.

'Let me see if any of our other surgeons are available. Trent Bagshaw might be able to help you.'

Trent was between cases in Theatre. Jennifer repeated her request, hoping that this third attempt might be luckier.

'He's not here, I'm afraid,' the surgeon told her apologetically. 'I wish he was. I'm totally snowed under with this case load. We've got a contract all set for him to sign but he said he'd make his decision after the conference.'

'Oh, I'd forgotten about the conference. It's in Miami, isn't it?'

'That's right. Half the department is there for the week. That's why I've been left with all the work. I'll have to go and get scrubbed again now. Nice talking with you, Jennifer.'

'Just a second,' Jennifer pleaded. 'Could you give Andrew a message for me, please? It's very important.'

'Sure. Fire away.'

'Tell him...' Jennifer's mind went blank. There was too much to say and none of it could be said to a stranger who had no time to wait. 'Just tell him I rang,' Jennifer said desperately. 'And...and give him my love.'

CHAPTER TEN

SURELY the call would be returned.

Andrew presumably wouldn't receive the message until after he returned from Miami. Jennifer calculated as best she could when that was likely to occur. Her level of tension rose markedly as that time came and went with no response. The days crawled past with exaggerated length. The ringing of the telephone, especially at odd hours in the night, had Jennifer's pulse racing, but the calls were never international. Old Mr Bates with the prostate problems had a heart attack. Mrs Dobson died peacefully in her sleep and Melissa Cooper chose exactly three a.m. the following Monday to go into labour.

The delivery was straightforward and efficient, but Jennifer had had very little sleep so it wasn't the ideal day to face the interviews for applicants vying for the position of her partner. She made herself a very strong cup of coffee at seven a.m., having left Melissa and her new daughter to rest under the care of the midwife, Sue. Considering the day ahead of her, Jennifer felt more than weary. Dispirited was a more accurate description. She would have to cope with her inpatients and any administrative tasks between the interviews. There were bound to be urgent appointments that would have to be slotted in somehow. It was just as well that Brian was going to be here for the day to help run the interviews.

Not that it should be a difficult process. Jennifer already had her hopes pinned on the married couple that were applying for the position. Two doctors for the price of one. She'd be able to cut her ties in the very near future and start again somewhere else. Boston, hopefully, but even the prospect of being with Andrew couldn't dispel Jennifer's weariness. The Drs Grant might be perfect but it would still take time for them to move to Akaroa and settle into the position. And Brian's surgery was still a week away. There was no way Jennifer was going to leave the country until he was firmly on the road to recovery.

Akaroa had chosen to advertise itself with perfect spring weather. The cloudless sky was reflected on a harbour that looked like blue silk. Fishing boats positioned themselves in picturesque fashion and Jennifer wouldn't have been at all surprised if a pod of Hector's dolphins was waiting to appear and charm any visitors. Not that the first visitor to the hospital that morning appeared to have noticed.

Katherine Hodderston arrived an hour early for her nine a.m. interview. She had been nervous about how long the drive from Christchurch would take, she said, and how hard it might be to find the hospital. The smart suit the young woman was wearing and the brand-new briefcase she carried looked out of place, but Jennifer had already known that this interview would probably be a waste of time. Katherine was only three years out of medical school. She was inexperienced, nervous and far too young. Brian had been the one who'd decided she deserved the courtesy of an interview.

'You were pretty young yourself when you started here,' he reminded Jennifer. 'And look what a treasure you turned out to be.'

Brian had to agree after the interview that Dr Hodderston wasn't suitable, but he remained philosophical. 'The next one will be better. Colin Draper sounds perfect on paper. He's thirty-six so he's definitely not too young. He's had plenty of GP experience and he has an interest in minor surgery.' Brian's eyebrows lifted meaningfully. 'Not bad-looking either, judging by this photograph.'

Colin Draper was certainly not bad-looking. Tall and lean with blond hair, blue eyes and a ready smile that would have prompted many women to take another look. Jennifer wasn't remotely attracted but Colin Draper clearly didn't share her lack of interest.

'*You're* Dr Tremaine?' The handshake was being extended a fraction too long. 'I didn't realise just how attractive this position really was.'

Jennifer pulled her hand free. 'What is it about the position that interested you, Colin?'

He waved a hand towards the window. 'This is such an amazing place. Not too far from a major city but with all the benefits of a seaside resort.' The blue eyes caught Jennifer's watchful stare and Colin smiled warmly. 'Do you know, I think I even saw dolphins in the harbour as I drove past?'

It transpired that Dr Draper was a keen sailor and wanted to live close to a yacht mooring. He was also recently divorced.

'Time for a new beginning,' he declared, his gaze resting appreciatively on Jennifer. 'And I can't wait to get started.'

'No,' Jennifer said firmly. 'He's not suitable at all.'

Wendy looked disappointed. 'I rather liked him.'

'So did I.' Brian poured himself a second cup of tea. 'And his qualifications are impeccable.' He grinned at Jennifer. 'He liked *you*.'

Jennifer snorted softly. 'He's certainly on the hunt for more than a job. I suspect he wants a deckhand for that yacht.'

The phone rang and Brian picked up the kitchen extension. 'Akaroa hospital,' he said pleasantly. 'Brian Wallace speaking.' His gaze was on Jennifer as he spoke and she watched to see if she could read anything urgent in his expression. Brian listened in silence for a few seconds and then spoke calmly. 'Hang on just a minute. I'll transfer the call to the office.' He pushed a button on the telephone and hung up. Then he picked up his cup of tea. 'Personal call,' he said casually. 'I'll be in the office.'

Wendy watched him leave before turning to Jennifer. 'Are you sure about Colin Draper?'

'Quite sure,' Jennifer responded.

'Shame,' Wendy said wistfully. 'I like sailing.'

Jennifer grinned at her friend. They shared a companionable few minutes finishing their lunches, then Jennifer carried her dishes to the bench. 'I'll be in the office as well,' she informed Wendy. 'We've got the last interview coming up and I'm sure this couple will be a far better prospect than Dr Draper.'

One glance out of the office window had Jennifer moving towards the front door with some speed. Some holidaymakers had arrived and Jennifer would need to deal with them quickly. She didn't want to be distracted from the interview that promised to solve the partnership problems.

The vast, bright green house truck was filling the car park. Garlands of flowers were painted on the sides amidst trees and rainbows. There were children running everywhere, totally undisciplined. Three small girls were picking all the flowers they could find in the garden. Two older boys were taking pot shots at a telegraph pole with stones they were collecting from the driveway. The two adults stood hand in hand, gazing serenely at the hospital entrance. The man was tall, bearded and had long hair tied back in a ponytail. The woman had loose, waist-length hair and wore a long dress that did not disguise the fact she was heavily pregnant.

'Can I help?'

'I doubt it. I think our prayers have already been answered.' The man took his eyes off the hospital long enough to smile happily at Jennifer.

'Oh?' Jennifer glared at the stone-throwing boys. They exchanged a knowing glance, grinned at each other and continued their game. 'Do you need medical attention for one of the children?'

'No.' The woman also smiled at Jennifer. 'We look after our children ourselves. We're both doctors.'

'Really?' Jennifer tried to ignore the alarm bells. Maybe it was just a horrible coincidence. She eyed the woman hopefully. Perhaps the arrival of yet another child was imminent. 'Did you need some attention yourself?' she queried politely. 'You look like you're not far off your delivery date.'

The woman laughed with genuine amusement. 'I've never needed help with childbirth yet and, goodness knows, I've had enough practice! But we do want to see a doctor. Two of them, in fact. Dr Wallace and Dr Tremaine.'

'I'm Dr Tremaine. Jennifer Tremaine.' There was no avoiding the sensation of total dismay now. The couple were positively beaming at her.

'I'm Peter Grant,' the bearded man told her.

'And I'm Bethany,' the woman added. 'We've come for our interview as your new partners.' She linked her arm with her husband's. 'And I know already that it's going to be absolutely perfect.'

*   *   *

By the time Jennifer was alone in the office with Brian more than an hour later she was trying very hard not to appear shell-shocked.

'It could be a good idea, having a married couple. One of them would always be available.' Jennifer searched for something positive to say about the Grants. 'They're very enthusiastic.'

'Very,' Brian agreed drily. 'Shame the enthusiasm doesn't extend to keeping their children under control. We'll have to get someone in to fix that window this afternoon.'

'Some people might appreciate their holistic approach to general practice,' Jennifer continued doggedly. 'I'm sure Peter would find a few customers for acupuncture. Maybe even for the homeopathy.'

'I don't think Bethany's ideas of natural childbirth and transcendental meditation will be highly sought after.'

'But their CVs are excellent. They're both competent GPs and they're very keen to get involved with the community. We have our share of alternative lifestylers. Bethany is already planning weaving classes and a support group for home schooling.'

'I thought you might be going to offer them the use of your house while they found the land for their herb farm.'

Jennifer grinned. She knew perfectly well she wasn't going to win this battle. She didn't even want to. 'They'll need accommodation for quite a while if they're going to build their house out of hand-made sod bricks.' She sighed. 'Still, it would have been ideal. A married couple that were both doctors and both keen to live in the area for good.'

'Ideal,' Brian agreed. 'If we take on Colin Draper, I imagine that's what we'd have just as soon as he could possibly manage it.' Brian grinned. 'Provided you co-operated, of course.'

'I have no intention of co-operating. I have no interest in Colin Draper. He's totally unsuitable as a partner. Professionally or otherwise.'

'His CV is even better than the Grants' and he's just as keen.'

'That's the problem. I have no intention of spending my working hours fending off un-wanted advances. I'm not interested in Colin Draper.'

'He might grow on you.'

'Like fungus.' Jennifer grinned again. 'Still, I suppose it might work out.' She bit her lip, hoping that what she was about to suggest wouldn't upset Brian. 'I may not stay here my-self once the new partner is settled and you're fit to supervise again.'

Brian didn't seem upset in the least. 'You wouldn't be thinking of going to Boston, would you?'

'I hope that might be a possibility,' Jennifer admitted a little shyly. 'It's not that I want to leave Akaroa but—'

'I understand perfectly,' Brian said with a smile. 'You don't have to explain anything.'

'It might not work out,' Jennifer added. 'It could be that I'm hunting something I've lost for ever. So maybe I'll end up staying here after all.'

Brian was still smiling. Jennifer was re-lieved that she hadn't upset him, but the relief was tinged with puzzlement. He wasn't at all bothered. In fact, he looked almost serene. Maybe some of the Grants' abundant positive energy had rubbed off on him.

'You never know what you'll find when you go hunting,' he told her. 'I suspect things will work out just perfectly. Right now, we need to concentrate on hunting down a partner for this practice.'

'The choice isn't that great, is it? I expected a lot more applicants than we got.'

'There is one more.' Brian checked his watch. 'The shuttle bus from Christchurch airport is due in five minutes so I'd better go. I said I'd collect him.'

'You didn't say anything about a late applicant. Where's the CV? What's his name?'

'It's all on the computer somewhere. Came by e-mail.' Brian was halfway through the door. 'See you soon.'

Jennifer could find nothing that looked like a CV or even an application for the position on the computer. She spent a good ten minutes searching and then gave up. Judging by the day so far, CVs and photographs weren't that helpful. There was no way of telling without a personal interview, but Jennifer was ready to give up the whole business—at least for now. When Wendy appeared to tell her that Brian was sending in the new applicant, Jennifer merely nodded.

'Is Brian coming in as well?'

'He'll be a few minutes.' Wendy was staring at Jennifer with an odd expression. Was she disappointed that Jennifer seemed so jaded? 'He's just waiting for Ruby to finish icing the chocolate cake so he can bring some in with the coffee.' Wendy was now avoiding Jennifer's gaze and staring at her own feet.

Jennifer nodded again. Brian had already had a chance to size up the new applicant alone. It was probably a good idea for her to have the same opportunity. 'Send him in, thanks, Wendy. Oh, hang on! What's his name?'

But Wendy had disappeared with remarkable alacrity. The odd sound of a muffled giggle kept Jennifer's gaze on the empty doorway. The figure that filled the space kept her gaze firmly locked into place.

'The name's Andrew,' the newcomer announced. 'Andrew Stephenson.'

'Drew!' The name came out as a stunned gasp. Jennifer rose slowly to her feet without even realising she was doing so. 'Come in. What on earth are *you* doing here?'

'I've come about the partnership,' Andrew stated. 'I'm applying for the position.'

'You're not!'

'Don't you want me to?' Andrew asked quietly. 'Have you found someone more suitable?'

'No—of course not.' Jennifer was still trying to muster some semblance of normal thought processes. 'But...but what about Boston?'

'Boston isn't what I want. I knew that almost the instant I arrived, but I was stuck. The court case got delayed. And I was having trouble trying to think of some way of persuading you that you didn't mean it when you told me not to come back. I was talked into attending that conference but when I got back and found your message waiting, that was all I needed. I got the first flight I could and I rang as soon as I landed. Brian answered the phone. He told me about the interviews today and suggested that we keep my arrival a surprise. He said he had the feeling that you'd welcome a late application.'

Jennifer felt perilously close to tears. She was at a complete loss for words. She needed time to adjust to having Andrew so close. There was too much that needed to be said, and for the life of her she couldn't think how to begin. This all seemed unreal. Fragile. If Andrew touched her right now she might break into a million pieces. Could he understand how stunned her emotions were? That she needed just a little time? He seemed to. He was watching her very carefully. He smiled and raised the large carrier bag he was holding.

'I bought some stuff for the kids,' he said casually. 'Twin dolls for Jess and Sophie. A computer game that Mike will love, and a fluffy yellow duck for Angus.'

'The children aren't here any more.' So much had changed in the short time since Andrew had left. Had what they'd had between them changed as well? 'They've gone to live in Australia with their father.'

'What?' Andrew sounded dismayed. 'When did that happen?'

'A couple of weeks ago.'

'I thought Philip was only coming to visit. Did you know about this before I left?' Andrew was disconcerted now. His expression was guarded.

'Of course not. In fact, it's because of you they've gone.'

'You mean you sent them away? You were planning to come to Boston after all?' Andrew shook his head. 'I hope you didn't. That's not what I wanted at all.'

'No. I mean yes.' Jennifer shook her head in confusion. The movement helped. Suddenly the words seemed to be there and they came rushing out. 'Yes, I was planning to come to Boston but I only decided that after the children had gone. It was entirely unexpected that Philip wanted to take them. And, no, I didn't send them away. It was that phone call that did it. The one when I told you Philip sounded jealous of how much the kids were talking about you. Philip *was* jealous. He didn't want anyone else stepping into his shoes and it prompted him into really thinking about his future. He bought a house and looked into schools and so on. Even then he wasn't planning to take them yet. He was just going to plant the suggestion and let them get used to the idea.'

'So what changed?' Andrew took a step closer. Jennifer was almost ready to touch him. To convince herself that he was real. Talking to him like this made her feel as though nothing had changed between them. He would listen and he would understand how she might feel.

'The kids weren't going to let him go unless they went, too. Even Zippy and the kitten have gone. The twins wanted to take Button but that wasn't on. They'll have to wait till their Christmas visit to ride him again. Philip's planning to bring the new woman in his life, Anne, on that visit as well.'

'How do you feel about that? Someone stepping into *your* shoes?'

'I couldn't be happier,' Jennifer said sincerely. 'I look forward to meeting her. It would have been very sad if Philip had clung to the past and his memories and not found someone to share his present and his future.'

Andrew took another step towards her. He looked very serious. 'Can I share your present, Jen? And your future?' His gaze was locked on hers. Jennifer managed to swallow the lump in her throat but it was still hard to speak.

'If I can share yours.'

'Can I make the assumption that I've been successful in my application to be your partner, Dr Tremaine?'

'I think so.' Jennifer hid a tremulous smile and tried to adopt a professional tone. 'I doubt very much that we could find a more suitable applicant for this position.' She held out her hand. 'Welcome to the practice, Mr Stephenson.'

Andrew shook her hand solemnly. 'I think I'll go back to being ''Dr'',' he told her. 'More suitable for a partner in general practice, I think.' He hadn't let go of her hand. 'However, it wasn't my professional application I was referring to.'

'Oh?' Jennifer didn't try to withdraw her hand. The electricity was still there. She couldn't have pulled away to save herself. Was Andrew pulling her closer or was she making the movement all by herself?

'My application for the position of partner in a much more personal arena was of more immediate interest. Will you still marry me, Jen? As soon as we can collect up our wedding party, of course. Will you marry me at Christmastime?'

'Of course I will.' The gap between them closed completely and Jennifer welcomed the touch of Andrew's lips on her own. She gave herself up to the kiss with a sigh of pure joy. The only thing that had changed was that any doubts either of them might have had had been erased. They belonged together. For ever. The perfect partnership. Jennifer wanted to give Andrew the same gift she had received. 'Are you sure about this, Drew?' She pulled away just enough to be able to see his face clearly.

'I could go to Boston. Or anywhere. It doesn't matter as long as we're together.'

'You couldn't go to Boston. Or anywhere else.' Andrew's fingers gently brushed the hair back from Jennifer's face. He kissed her forehead. 'You belong here, Jennifer Tremaine.' He kissed her nose. 'With your family history and home and a community that loves you.' He kissed her lips. 'I want to belong, too.'

'You do,' Jennifer said softly. 'We belong together.'

'Partners,' Andrew said with satisfaction. 'Permanent partners.'

Jennifer smiled her agreement just before Andrew's lips claimed hers yet again.

'Perfect partners,' she murmured. Jennifer wound her arms around the neck of the man she loved. She had no intention of saying anything else for quite some time.